Gertrude & The Sorcerer's Gold

The Gumboot & Gumshoe Series:

Book Four

By

Laura Hesse

Running L. Productions   Vancouver Island, B.C.

Gertrude & The Sorcerer's Gold
COPYRIGHT© 2020 Laura Hesse

The author and the publisher make no representation, express or implied, with regard to the accuracy of the information contained in this book. The material is provided for entertainment purposes and the references are intended to be supportive to the intent of the story. The author and the publisher are not responsible for any action taken based on the information provided in this book.

All characters in this publication, other than those clearly in the public domain, are fictitious and any resemblance to real persons, living or dead, is purely coincidental.

National Library of Canada Cataloguing in Publication Data
Hesse, Laura - 1959
Gertrude & The Sorcerer's Gold/by Laura Hesse
ISBN Print: 978-1-9990774-2-6
ISBN e-book: 978-1-9990774-3-3

Cover Design: Copyright 2020 Laura Hesse
Cover Artist: Autumn Sky, Self Pub Book Covers Inc.
Publisher: Running L. Productions, Vancouver Island, British Columbia, Canada
Website: *Running L Productions*

Forward

While it helps if you have read the first three books in the series (*Gumboots, Gumshoes and Murder, The Dastardly Mr. Deeds* and *Murder Most Fowl*) to understand the characters and their relationships, this story is designed as a standalone so don't worry if you haven't read about this crazy cast yet.

Gumboots, Gumshoes and Murder was the first book in *The Gumboot and Gumshoe Series* followed by *The Dastardly Mr. Deeds* and *Murder Most Fowl*. These novels need to be read in order.

Gertrude & The Sorcerer's Gold was inspired by actual events. Brother Twelve was a rogue profit who during the 1920's began a journey that resulted in the formation of The Aquarian Society in 1927 in Nanaimo, British Columbia. He was the first spiritualist to welcome in the Age of Aquarius and even predicted the Stock Market Crash in the 1930's as well as World War II. I have included some links at the back of the book if you want to learn more about the life of Brother Twelve.

Enjoy.

Contents

Quote 1

1933 2

Present Day 5

Double Trouble 13

Double Eagle 23

Tempest in a Tea Pot..34

Things That Go Bump in the Night 46

Knock Three Times 55

The Emancipation of Tammy Smith..............................68

Break and Enter 82

Pig Hunt..94

Gold Fever 114

Powder..136

Oscars, Flashers, and Old Lace....................................153

Old McDonald's Farm 171

Saint Bernard's & Sister Fate..181

Prophets & Prophecies..197

Desolation Sound 205

Interesting Links – More on Brother XII 210

Novels by Laura Hesse..211

About the Author 212

Gertrude & The Sorcerer's Gold

Quote

"Gold conjures up a mist about a man, more destructive of all his old senses and lulling to his feelings than the fumes of charcoal."

— Charles Dickens, Nicholas Nickleby

1933

The stars in the Milky Way shone like diamonds in the cloudless sky. A full moon illuminated the giant Red cedar, Sitka spruce and Douglas fir trees that marched up the steep slopes of the island to the crest of Watchtower Mountain.

Waves broke on the rocky beach, the water making a shushing sound as if it was telling the night birds to hush.

A large tugboat, its silhouette black against the glow cast from the moon on the water, was anchored offshore. Two lanterns, one on the bow and one on the stern, cast minimal shadows on the secret endeavors of the boat's crew. The name on the bronze plaque on the bow read Kheunaten.

A wiry middle-aged man with dark bronzed skin, a smattering of white hair amid his blue-black locks and bush of a beard, along with his companion, climbed out of a wooden hulled dingy. His companion was a short dark-haired woman with a stern countenance. They carried two heavy wooden boxes between them, two feet wide by two feet long and two feet deep, one balanced on top of the other. The woman staggered under the weight.

"Don't drop it," the man growled.

"Don't be stupid, of course I won't," she snarled back.

The pair carried the boxes up a slope and into the forest.

"Here. Put it here," the man ordered once they reached the tall tree that bordered the edge of a small meadow.

The woman gratefully placed the boxes on the ground. The soft tinkle of glass rubbing on glass was heard, the sound muffled by the wooden sides of the crates. The woman looked up into the dense foliage of the Garry oak tree, the leaves so thick that they blocked out the moonlight. She lost her balance for a moment.

"Are you sure we'll be able to find it again," she hissed, reaching for the tree trunk for support.

"I know where I am," he whispered hoarsely.

"That's not what I asked," she retorted, agitated.

The man ignored her and returned to the dingy.

The woman stood alone in the meadow. She shivered despite the warmth of the night. The dark that surrounded her was absolute; so intense that it was claustrophobic. The moonlight was barely able to penetrate the dense stands of deciduous and evergreen trees that bordered the meadow. Most of the trees were taller than the oak under which she stood. There were no signs of civilization anywhere on this side of the island.

The man returned with a shovel and began to dig. He dug a hole wide enough for the two boxes to lay side-by-side. The gravel and rock-strewn topsoil were too difficult to dig deeper. The first box landed inside the hole with a loud thump. Once again, the jingle of glass was heard, much like the sound of silver bells, each note echoing prettily in the quiet solitude of the meadow. The second box landed on top of the first, the sound deadened by the wood planking the boxes were made of.

"What if something happens to you," she said. Her voice was husky and demanding. "I need to be able to find this Godforsaken place."

"Fine," he mumbled.

He took his shovel and carved an eye inside a triangle in the rough bark of the Garry oak tree.

"Satisfied?"

"But where exactly are we?"

"Where it was foretold," he groused and stalked off.

The woman looked around and then trotted after him, her boots crunching on the gravel as she left the shelter of the forest to stumble across the beach towards the waiting dingy.

She stopped to stare at the moon. It reminded her of a glass Christmas globe. She then gazed intently at the slightly squared off top of Watchtower Mountain, burning the image into her memory until she was sure that she could recognize it again.

"Hurry up," her companion snarled, pushing the dingy into the water.

"I'm coming, Brother," she soothed him.

The woman climbed into the boat and then the man pushed the dingy away from the shore. He vaulted over the side like a man much younger than his fifty years.

"I'm sorry if I offended you, my dear," she purred.

"You didn't my love," he replied, his voice cracking.

"Let them all be damned."

The woman laughed.

After a moment so did the man.

Present Day

"Oh, Gertie, do stay out of trouble," retired Supreme Court Judge Violet Bone said, wagging a finger at the grey and white pot-bellied pig.

"You too, Peaches," silver haired Archie Bruce warned the cream-colored Jersey cow.

The pig squinted through the folds of fat that half covered her eyes, her inquisitive look darkening at being unceremoniously escorted out of the kitchen and onto the back porch.

The cow stood in the yard nibbling on the seeds within a gloriously large and brilliant yellow sunflower, a perpetual look of confusion on its face.

A blush crept over the woman's cheeks as she looked up into the cheeky sparkle in the eyes of her companion. The two returned to the cottage and closed the door on the annoyed pig.

"You did remember to lock the front gate didn't you," the woman whispered as the door clicked shut.

"Don't I always," the man's baritone voice rumbled.

"No," the woman whispered huskily.

A series of girlish giggles and the stomp of feet across a hardwood floor was all that Gertrude heard after that.

Tea and cookie time were over.

Gertrude was getting used to being shunted outside.

Gertrude's hooves clattered on the wood planking as she waddled off the porch and down the cobblestone lane leading to the drive.

Her buddy mooed pathetically, not wanting to leave the garden full of sunflowers.

Gertrude snorted, her nostrils quivering.

She was irked.

Gertrude toddled down the driveway, her curvaceous body jiggling as she walked towards the gate. She stopped and checked over her shoulder. Despite the call of the sunflowers, Peaches followed her friend, her teeth working the sunflower seeds in her mouth into mulch. The pig grunted in satisfaction.

The two animals had always been friends but were inseparable now that RCMP Sergeant Betty Bruce had retired and moved back to Seal Island permanently. Betty had adopted Peaches after Andy McDowell had willed his house to Betty shortly before he died. Gertrude was supposed to stay with Betty's father, Archie, but she preferred to live with Peaches, and no one seemed put out by it.

Gertrude ambled off in search of a human friend with a handful of dog biscuits or a pint of beer that they were willing to part with.

The gate at the end of the driveway stood open.

The pot-bellied pig sniffed the air, her mind whirring. She looked first right towards the pub and marina, and then left towards the McDonald's farm. Rainbow

McDonald always had dog biscuits to spare, but Stew Mann, the owner of The Bristling Boar pub, might offer her a dram of beer now that his mean wife was gone.

Gertrude was a smart pig. She only stayed with Archie and Violet when Betty and Reggie were off cruising on Reggie's boat. It hadn't taken the pig long to figure that out. Without Reggie, the likelihood of a shared beer with a stranger at the pub was remote, and Stew was predictably unpredictable, much like Gertrude herself.

North Shore Road wasn't paved. None of the roads on Seal Island were. Heat waves shimmered over the packed gravel and dirt. The grass at the side of the road was coated with dust and burnt brown from the summer sun. Whatever she decided, it would be a long hot walk. Beer was her preference, but Milk Bones were a good second.

That settled it.

The pig trotted up the road with thoughts of Milk Bones twirling around and around in her head. Where Gertrude went, Peaches followed, and so the cow did.

That one choice, made by a pot-bellied pig in the heat of the day, the decision to choose Milk Bones over beer, triggered a series of calamitous events that would haunt Seal Island for decades to come.

***

Gertrude walked with her head down, a thin strand of drool dripping from her mouth, into the McDonald's farmyard. The noon day sun beat down upon the pot-bellied pig and the Jersey cow.

Gertrude yearned for a mud bath to protect her skin from the blistering summer sun. Peaches had no idea what she yearned for; she lived for the moment.

The air was hazy and still. A thin layer of wispy cloud hovered above the top of Watchtower Mountain making the mountain's normally vibrant green forest look dull.

Gertrude and Peaches wandered down the driveway. The water fountain in front of the small log cabin gurgled like a baby blowing spit bubbles. Bees buzzed. Water striders skipped along the top of the dark water between the lily pads.

The pig dove into the little pond.

Lily pads cascaded over the fountain's paver stone border.

The cow stopped for a much-needed drink.

The McDonald's Blue Heeler ran towards them, tongue lolling. It first nosed the cow to say 'hello' and then dove into the fountain alongside the pig, barking furiously. Water flew everywhere.

Rainbow, her auburn and blond streaked dreadlocks pulled back under a multi-colored scarf, stopped picking herbs in the fenced off garden and shaded her eyes from the sun to see what was causing all the commotion. She laughed when she saw the heeler and the pot-bellied pig cavorting in the ornamental pond.

Frank sat aboard a tractor in the far fields, his focus fixed on the task at hand. The tractor's revolving blades growled as they turned over the dry ground, the engine humming, metal screeching when it hit rock. Dust hung thick in the air behind the man and his machine.

The McDonalds one farm hand, a pretty young woman with a mane of peach colored hair and a sparkling personality, stepped out of the barn, a tin of pop in her hand. She too laughed when she saw the pig and dog in the fountain.

Melanie went back into the barn and returned with a couple of Milk Bones and a long-stemmed carrot.

Rainbow grinned and waved to her. She then returned to work, clipping thyme and pruning sage.

"You guys give new meaning to The Three Musketeers," Melanie chuckled.

Gertrude and Blue stopped playing. Blue jumped out of the pond and vigorously shook himself off. Gertrude snorted and lay down in the water for another roll.

"Here you go, Peaches," Melanie said, handing the cow the carrot. The cow gently took the treat from the tanned woman's hand. She then kissed Peaches on the soft swirl of hair between her eyes.

The dog sat obediently, his blue grey and black coat glistening in the sunshine.

"Good boy, Blue," handing the dog a Milk Bone. The dog gently took it from her.

Gertrude stood up, her curly tail wind milling furiously. She grunted and snorted but refused to come out of the water.

"I'm not going in after you just to give you a Milk Bone if that's what you're thinking," Melanie chortled, holding out the treat.

Gertrude sighed, disappointed.

Melanie burst out laughing.

"Come on, out you come, or I'll go and fetch a broom."

Gertrude eyed her dubiously, but hauled her great heft upwards and leaned forward, trying to nip the Milk Bone from Melanie's outstretched hand.

"Oh, no, you don't. All the way out, you cheeky pig," Melanie cajoled the errant animal.

Gertrude snorted in disgust and stepped out of the pond, a lily pad sucker root wound around her tail.

Melanie handed Gertrude the biscuit and patted her gently on the forehead.

"Ooh, but you stink, Gertie. I would love to visit with you, but I have work to do and everyone else is working as well so off you go."

Gertrude understood the tone of Melanie's voice and walked past her, farting as she did so.

"I'll remember that the next time you want a treat," Melanie glowered, waving a hand in front of her face.

The pig cast a sad look the girl's way and then waddled past her, hooves clicking on the meandering pebbled path that lead down to the ocean. Peaches followed the pot-bellied pig; the Blue Heeler followed the cow. The dog's tail wagged furiously from side to side.

Melanie's sweet laugh echoed through the still air as she walked back to the barn.

Gertrude followed her nose. The tangy scent of salt water intermingled with the rancid smell of rotting seaweed urged her on. She regularly found tasty treats nestled within the seaweed, like the wonderful old sneaker with the severed foot inside that she found last year. She had been really irritated when Betty and Archie had taken it away from her. Today there were no humans to wrestle any prize finds away from her.

Gertrude and her entourage emerged onto the sandy shore. The tide was in which didn't bode well for beachcombing.

The dog was happy though. It barged past her and galloped into the water.

A couple of seagulls paddled by; yellow eyes forever watchful.

The dog barked and chased after the gulls.

The cow munched on the sea asparagus that grew in the moist areas along the shore.

The air was still with hardly a breath of wind rippling the waters of the Strait of Georgia between the British Columbia mainland and the rocky coast of Seal Island.

Gertrude's bristling hair was already dry from her swim in the pond and her skin was beginning to burn. The cool shade of the forest was only a short distance away. That appealed to her more than the open beach.

The dog whined as it watched the pig stroll across the beach and into the forest. The cow quickly trotted after it. The dog, knowing it wasn't allowed to go any farther, spun around and galloped back the way it had come, leaving the pig and cow to their wanderings.

***

A small cabin was built into the side of a rocky shoal. The back of the building was a wall of rock. The front opened onto a patchwork quilt of light and dark thanks to the shade of a giant Garry oak tree. The oiled parchment that covered the cabin's front windows was yellow and cracked with age. The sod roof was thick with tall sedge grass. The door canted sideways, one of its hinges broken.

Gertrude stuck her snout through the partially opened door and inhaled deeply. The smell of rot and mould greeted her. Nothing of interest there. She pulled her head back out of the building and moseyed over to the base of the old oak tree.

Peaches mooed and climbed the steep bank. She walked onto the roof of the cabin and began to devour the lush green grasses that grew there. The old logs creaked under the cow's weight but miraculously held fast.

The pig snuffled around the base of the tree. A rotting black ball of truffle popped out of the earth. Gertrude ate it swiftly.

She rooted around for more, digging and digging with her sharp cloven hooves. If there was one, there must be more.

Gertrude squealed in pain as something hard caught between her toes. She tried to dislodge it with her mouth, but whatever it was, was wedged in tight. She stomped a foot, but that only lodged the painful thing in deeper.

She stumbled forward.

Gertrude's eyes watered. The thing caught between her toes was excruciatingly painful.

Peaches looked up. She saw Gertrude limping away, and then turned back to the shoots of lush green grass on the roof. She didn't want to leave it.

Gertrude shambled through the small meadow and turned left onto the deer trail that wound its way onto South Shore Road. She wanted Betty... or Reggie... or Archie to fix it. They were the only people she trusted, especially after witnessing her best friend, Peaches, get shot with a taser by an evil man.

Eventually Peaches realized that Gertrude was gone. She bellowed loudly. When Gertrude didn't answer, she jogged down the embankment and trotted in the direction that she had last seen her buddy go.

Double Trouble

Pearl Tullis prided herself in being able to live independently despite her failing eyesight. Her shoulders, though bent, were still strong after eighty-nine years on this planet called Earth. Her hands and arms were speckled with age spots. She had seen a lot over the years and was happiest in her garden or in the company of the fellow members of the Seal Island Vagabond Writer's Society.

Pearl was a poet, or at least she tried to be. She knew she wasn't much of a wordsmith, but she wrote with passion and elegance. She raged at growing old, of dreams unfulfilled, and the follies of youth.

She loved the Writer's Society, but it wasn't the same without Tiffany to guide it. The members still met once a week for book discussions. Pearl was ever thankful to her grandson for showing her how to use the internet to download audio books that she could listen to at her leisure now that she couldn't read at all.

Pearl and her husband had been pioneers. They were one of the original couples to clear land and build a home on Seal Island. She still lived in the house that they had built over fifty years ago.

Though she loved her old house, it wasn't without its flaws. The back door to the kitchen stood wide open. The air outside, though hot, was still cooler than the insufferable heat in the kitchen.

Pearl had two loaves of bread in the oven so that she wouldn't have to make any more for a few days. Her granddaughter had bought her a bread maker, but the box sat on the counter, still unopened. The day that she couldn't enjoy the simple pleasures of kneading the flour and smelling the yeast as it rose was the day that she would check herself into a senior's home.

Pearl hummed as she set a timer and then made her way out the back door into the garden.

The sweet scents of thyme and mint intermixed with the heady scent of a myriad of flowering rose bushes embraced her. Bees buzzed and hummingbirds hummed through-out the garden causing the old woman to pause, a thin-lipped smile lighting up her craggy features.

Every type of rose under the sun grew in Pearl's garden including a vibrant red climbing tea rose which wound up a cedar trellis beside the back door. Bright yellow Floribunda roses, pink Queen Elizabeth roses, and a host of colorful hybrids grew along her garden pathway and tumbled over the small white fence that bordered South Shore Road.

The old woman picked up the small wicker basket on the steps beside the kitchen door and took out the pruning shears. She then went to work on the bushes closest to the road so that she worked backwards towards the house in order to be able to hear the timer in the kitchen when it went off. She fingered each bush carefully, using scent and smell to guide her way. Every so often, Pearl miscalculated, and a thorn pierced her flesh, but a quick suck of the pin pricked finger and she was off again.

A snip here, and a snap there.

Pearl reveled in the sun beating down upon her back and her shoulders as she dead headed the bush in front of her. It warmed her bones and eased the arthritis that bent her back and crippled her knees.

She heard a rustling of clothing and what sounded like footsteps on the gravel road.

"Hello," she called to the traveler, "beautiful day, isn't it?"

The footsteps came closer.

She wasn't expecting anyone, but it was summer, and tourists loved to stroll the island. Sometimes, if they were interested in history, she would invite them in for tea and regale them with stories from her past.

Pearl wasn't completely blind. She saw movement and color. Right now, the world was a patchwork quilt of dappled sunlight and vibrant rainbows, the different hues blending into an artist palette of red, blue, yellow, and purple. The forest across the road looked like a cathedral of grey and green. She was due to have cataract surgery next month and was determined not to cancel it for the umpteenth time.

"Gertrude is that you," she asked, sensing something or someone was there…watching her. If not the pig, then who?

Still there was no answer.

No grunt.

No snort.

A tall willowy shadow stepped into the bright spray of sunlight directly in front of her.

Pearl gasped. The shadow was too big to be the pig and not big enough to be a cow.

"Who are you? What do you want?"

There was a rustle of clothes and the zip of a zipper as the shadow man stepped forward and appeared to rip open his shirt and undo his pants.

With a start, Pearl realized that she was in jeopardy. The thought of someone assaulting her in her rose garden was terrifying.

Who on earth would want to assault an old woman like her?

She wasn't pretty, never had been, nor had she aged well. That was one of the reasons she had been indifferent to losing her eyesight; it meant she didn't have to look at her reflection in the mirror anymore. Her husband, God bless him, hadn't married her because she was handsome, he married her because she was capable.

The shadow man stood in place. Something large and pink wiggled frantically between his legs.

Pearl snorted out a laugh when she realized what was happening.

"Are you flashing me," she cackled, wagging the sharp pruning shears in the man's face. "Or is it a wee diddle with an old woman you're looking for?"

Pearl continued to laugh as the man stood there. She sensed that her reaction wasn't the one that he had hoped for.

"You do realize that I'm blind as a bat, young man, and that I haven't had sex for damn near thirty years."

Still she received no answer.

"Come on then, which is it? Flash or diddle? I've got bread in the oven."

The man zipped up his zipper and fled down the road. The old woman's hoarse laughter reverberated in the air behind him.

"Ooh, I can't wait to tell the girls about this one," Pearl snickered as her timer went off in the kitchen.

***

Sadie Stewart opened the door to her sister's house. Tempest and her new husband were on a honeymoon cruise to Alaska.

She walked into the large foyer and looked around, her small Yorkie whisking in behind her. It was a beautiful *Gone with the Wind* house. A sweeping oak stairwell led to the upstairs bedrooms. She expected Scarlett O'Hara to appear at the top of the stairs in an illustrious ball gown at any minute.

Sadie had never really understood why Tempest had divorced Sam Garner. He had been devoted to her and had built the enormous southern style mansion for his demanding wife, despite Tempest's constant whining. Nothing was ever good enough for Tempest.

Sadie thought her sister was a spoiled brat. Not that Sadie didn't love her younger sister, but Tempest rarely thought of anyone else but Tempest. Tempest had cleaned the poor man out. It was cruel. Her sister had been aptly named in Sadie's opinion.

"Come on, Cindy," she said to the tiny dog, "time to do our rounds not that we'll ever receive a thank you for it."

Sadie walked through the house, her footsteps and the scratch of the Yorkie's tiny claws on marble echoing in the vast expanse. She checked the kitchen first, ran a bit of water through the taps, and opened the fridge to make sure there was no rotting food inside. She picked up an open carton of milk and sniffed it. It was still good, so she put it back.

The Yorkie's ears pricked up. The little dog growled.

She heard it to. There was a loud rattling sound coming from the upstairs bedroom above her head.

Sadie scooped up the dog and walked back into the grand foyer.

The rattle turned into a series of loud thumps.

The Yorkie yipped and shivered in her arms.

"I agree, kiddo, I'm not going up there by myself."

Sadie backed out of the house. She then closed and locked the door behind her.

The young mother ran home, the tiny dog bouncing in her arms.

She raced home, which thankfully was right next door, past her eight year-old son playing basketball with a friend in the yard, up the back porch stairs, through the open door into the house, past her six year-old daughter watching cartoons on the television in the living room, and into her studio where her cell phone lay charging on top of her desk.

Sadie flipped down the list of names in her address book until she found Betty Bruce's. She dialed her number, hoping that Betty was home and not out cruising somewhere with Reggie.

Betty's phone went straight to voice mail.

"Hey, Betty," she said nervously into the phone, "this is Sadie Stewart. I just checked Tempe's house and there are weird noises coming from upstairs. It sounds like someone is in the house. It doesn't sound like a racoon, more like someone rifling through stuff. Can you please come over and check it out for me? I'm alone with the kids. Mark is in camp. Thanks."

***

Betty sat on a white fold-up lawn chair on the deck of the thirty-five-foot former trawler, the *Persephone*, reading the latest John Grisham novel. A beige ball cap with the RCMP logo on it shaded her eyes. Her salty blond hair was cut in a short bob for the summer. She wore a white and blue checked blouse with a dime sized ketchup stain on the lapel, faded blue jean cut-offs, and leather Doctor Scholl sandals.

Betty was a handsome woman, her soft curves and intelligent, steady gaze making her both approachable and commanding at the same time. After twenty-six years as a member of the Royal Canadian Mounted Police, she had decided to take early retirement. Trouble, however, had a way of finding her. The RCMP had hired her as a Private Consultant. Her friends had christened her with their own title, that of very Special Agent Beatrice (Betty) Bruce.

The boat she was on belonged to Reggie Phoenix. It was his pride and joy. Reggie had spent ten years overhauling the 1935 wooden hulled ship. Its sides were painted a flat black, the trim fire truck red, and the deck was stained a golden oak color. The trawler had been in his family for years. He and his father had both worked on her when fishing licenses were passed down from father to son. Reggie had seen the writing on the wall and had converted the fishing trawler into a dive and tour boat when salmon stocks started to decline. The *Persephone* also made for a great smuggler's ship thanks to its black wooden hull.

The man in question, a reformed pot grower and retired fisherman, stood at the helm. The brass and steel gauges on the panel in front of him gleamed. Reggie's eyes were as deep and unfathomable as the grey sea on which he had spent his life. His face was tanned a deep mahogany. His grey and white hair was an unruly mop that refused to be tamed. He looked a lot like Nick Nolte.

Betty's newest partner, a German shepherd with a nose for all manner of drugs and explosives, lay on the floor beside Reggie. Champ had been sent to Rainbow McDonald for help in overcoming his fear of loud noises and crowds. It was a huge problem considering the dog worked at the Vancouver International Airport.

Champ had failed to overcome his issues, despite Rainbow's best efforts. He had also bonded so deeply with Betty that Rainbow suggested that Betty be allowed to adopt him. When the head officer found out who Betty was, he had quickly agreed.

Champ was a typical German shepherd. He rarely left Betty's side. His love and devotion to his pack leader was so great that he rose to the occasion when she needed him most, overcoming almost all of his fears and anxieties.

The other person the shepherd loved was the amiable and soft-hearted captain of the *Persephone*. Currently, the dog was comfortably snoozing on the cabin's floor, his head resting on Reggie's feet.

Sweat dripped from the cold can of beer in Reggie's hand and onto the dog's head, but the shepherd barely noticed.

Reggie watched the buoy markers, his eyes fixed on the channel as he steered the *Persephone* past Saturna Island heading south by southeast on the inside passage between the mainland and Vancouver Island towards Seal Island.

Seal Island was a pretty little piece of paradise off the coast of Vancouver Island. It was only accessible by passenger ferry, boat or seaplane. The population swelled during the summer, but the winters were left to only the hardiest of the island residents. That was how they liked it.

Reggie glanced over his shoulder at the woman he loved more than life itself. He smiled, the deep crow's feet around his eyes softening.

Betty sensed him looking and glanced up. She smiled into the kind and craggy face that regarded her with such open charm.

Betty's cell phone began to buzz. She looked down at the display. It read 'Private Caller'.

"Don't answer it," Reggie yelled, seeing her pick up the phone.

"I have to," she called back.

"No, ya don't," he said gruffly, throttling back the engine. "I'll turn us around if'n ya don't wait until we at least get home."

The dog looked from Reggie to Betty and then back again. He whined loudly.

"See, Champ agrees."

Betty laughed and put down the phone, leaving the call to go to voice mail.

"That's better," he said, nodding at the dog and revving up the big diesel engines once again. "Yer master's finally figuring out what retirement is all about."

The dog yawned and wagged its tail.

The phone rang yet again.

Betty fought the urge to pick it up and returned to her novel.

That only lasted a minute.

She picked up the phone, looked at the screen, two messages waited for her. She sighed tucked the phone inside the chair's built-in cupholder knowing instinctively that her beau was watching her every move from inside the wheelhouse.

He'd do it too…turn the boat around if she didn't stop fussing. He had done it once already.

Betty grinned crookedly and returned to the book for the last time.

Double Eagle

Archie and Vi sat in the pub at a table by the window. The Bristling Boar was hopping. The marina was full of pleasure craft. They outnumbered the fishing boats by six to one. Many more were moored out in the bay off the lighthouse.

Stew worked behind the bar filling drink orders while his two new waitresses were hopping from table to table in bebop movements the envy of the white-haired patrons scattered about the pub. The air smelled like fish and chips and beer.

"That looks like the *Persephone*," Violet said, pointing out the window to where a large trawler was puttering into view in the Strait.

"Hope Eddie kept Reggie's berth open," Archie replied, his brow knitting with worry.

"I think I see an opening to the left of the passenger ferry dock," Vi advised him.

"Hey, Archie, you better come quick," a red-haired Morris Tweedsmuir called from the doorway.

"Why," Archie shouted back, his voice barely heard over the din in the crowded pub.

"It's Gertie, she's here and it looks like she's hurt," Morris yelled.

Archie almost knocked his beer and burger flying as he leapt out of his seat and raced across the pub floor, dodging the waitresses and tourists alike. He brushed past Morris and ducked quickly out the door.

Gertrude limped down the sloping hill where South Shore Road joined North Shore Road, the two gravel roads intersecting at the pub and marina. Behind her trotted the Jersey cow.

"Gertie," Archie bellowed, bolting down the steps and across the road to meet the pig, Morris hot on his heels.

"Looks like she's hurt her left hoof," Morris said breathlessly.

The pig stopped. She leaned her head into Archie's thighs. Her intelligent eyes wept with pain.

"Oh, sweetie, what's happened to you," Archie asked the pig.

Gertrude grunted and snuffled his hand.

"If you hold her head, I'll lift the foot and see if I can find what's hurting her," Morris offered.

"Thanks, Morris," Archie replied.

Peaches ambled up behind her friend. She stopped beside the two men, checking them out as Morris bent over to lift Gertrude's hoof. While Peaches wasn't as smart as her cohort, she knew when something was wrong.

Morris grunted, his knees popping, the cartilage close to buckling as he bent down to pick up the pig's hoof, Gertrude's bulk leaning against his leg, nearly knocking him over. The pig out-weighed him by almost a hundred pounds.

A crowd gathered around them, Gertrude being the unofficial mascot of Seal Island and the subject of many an evening news story on global networks around the world. Her escapades on Seal Island were legendary.

"Is she okay, Archie," Vi asked, shouldering her way through the crowd of local fishermen and tourists. "Should I call the vet?"

"Not yet, honey," Archie responded. "Let's see if Morris can find what's bothering her."

Vi nodded in response, her brow furrowing and cheeks flushing with anger as several people pulled out their phones and started recording.

"I see what's bothering her," Morris said, trying to pry the object from between the pig's cloven hoof. "It's wedged in there pretty hard whatever it is."

"Anybody got a pair of pliers," Archie asked the fishermen gathered around them.

"I do," a gruff broad-shouldered man said, pulling a pair of needle nose pliers from his back pocket. "I was just fixing my motor. Good thing, eh?"

The crowd murmured its approval as the man handed Morris the pliers.

Morris lifted Gertrude's hoof back up and continued to work at the obstruction. The pig grunted and tried to head butt him, but Archie intervened.

All at once the object gave way and Morris flew backwards, landing with a hard thump on the ground.

The crowd cheered.

The pig put her foot down and took a couple of steps forward without limping.

"Well that did it," Archie grinned.

"Thank heavens for small mercies," Vi said.

"Will you look at this," Morris muttered, holding up what appeared to be a gold coin.

Archie took the coin from Morris' hand and examined the twenty-dollar gold piece. The Lady Liberty was on one side and a golden eagle in flight was on the other. The date on the coin was 1927.

"That looks like a St. Gaudin's double eagle," a tourist blurted out, trying to take the coin from Archie. "If it is, it's in remarkable shape."

Archie whisked the coin away and looked at it more closely. The gold coin gleamed in the sunlight.

"Whatever it is, Gertie found it, so I'll hold on to it until someone calls my daughter looking for it," Archie replied in a steely voice, brooking no argument.

"Strange that it's dated 1927," a fisherman stated, his friends nodding assent.

"Probably from someone's collection," another said.

"Then how'd it get in Gertrude's hoof," Morris wondered aloud. "Ya don't think it might be part of the Brother's treasure, do ya, Arch?"

"What treasure," someone else asked.

The crowd was growing in ever larger proportions as people posted the video of Morris lifting the coin from Gertrude's hoof on social media. Anyone in the area who saw it was rushing down to the landing.

"Why Brother Twelve's of course," Morris added.

"Who is Brother Twelve," several people asked at once.

"A strange fella from England," Morris replied. "He had a commune in the twenties on DeCourcy and Valdes Islands."

"One in Cedar by the Sea outside of Nanaimo too," Violet said. "I remember the story."

"He was a con man," the fisherman with the pliers said. "Swindled people out of all their money, converted it to gold coin, and then skipped out on them when they got wise to him."

"My grandfather did some work for Brother Twelve," Morris said, puffing up at the attention he was getting. "He told me that Brother Twelve and his lady, Madam Z, buried the boxes of coins all over the Gulf Islands. He moved them around a lot."

"And you think the pig found the treasure," someone yelled excitedly.

Vi frowned as more and more people started recording Morris, Gertrude and Archie on video.

"Archie, we need to get Gertrude and Peaches out of here," Vi whispered urgently in Archie's ear.

Archie too saw the escalation in the crowd's mood.

"Go get Betty and Reggie. The *Persephone's* docking," he whispered fiercely. "I'll try and get away from this lot."

Vi broke away from the crowd, walking quickly towards the dock.

"Come on, Gert, time to go," Archie mumbled, grabbing the pig by the ear and pulling her forward, trying to urge her up North Shore Road.

"Hey, we want to get a look at that coin," someone yelled from the back of the horde of men and women gathering about him in an ever-tightening circle.

"Yeah, come on, give us all a look," another called out.

Several people took that as a cue to try to boss Archie around, thinking the wiry silver haired senior a push over.

Morris tried to intervene but was shoved aside.

"Bugger off," Archie spat as he brushed off more and more grabbing hands.

A balding beer bellied brute leapt forward and spun Archie around. Archie staggered. The man fumbled for Archie's pocket, tearing the fabric as he reached in for the coin.

The fat man didn't get very far.

Gertrude charged, taking him out above the knees.

The pig tossed him around like a rag doll even though pound for pound, they were probably a match.

The cow panicked and rammed into the people too daft to get out of the way, so engrossed in filming the scene unfolding before them that they didn't move quick enough. A man fell against a woman, that woman tripped a teen, each person hitting someone else until the domino effect took out half of the mob. Peaches bellowed in fear and tried not to step on anyone before running for home.

Tempers flared!

Betty raced into the middle of the medley, the German shepherd at her side alternating between whining fearfully, tail between its leg, and barking furiously. The dog hated crowds, but as people scuttled out of the way, the shepherd grew more confident.

"Break it up NOW," Betty hollered, parting the crowd like Moses parted the Red Sea.

The German shepherd found its heart and leapt forward, dragging Betty with it. The dog snapped a warning at the balding beer bellied man still trying to manhandle Archie. The man pirouetted around the pig, his eyes glazed over with gold fever, and skipped aside, just missing a nip from the frenzied shepherd.

"Give me it," the bald man demanded. "I can tell you what it's worth."

"Sod off, buddy, I don't care what it's worth," Archie yelled. "It ain't yours. It's going to the cops."

Gertrude's eyes blazed; snot dripped from her flattened nostrils.

"Keep that pig away from me. She's a killer. She touches me and I'll have her turned into bacon. That dog too. He draws blood and he's dead."

That set Morris and the local fishermen off. They barged forward.

"Get your bloody hands off my father or my pig is the least of your worries," Betty demanded, holding the fisherman back with one pointed look. "I don't know what this is about, but it ends here!"

"Ya touch either of them and ya all will answer ta me," Reggie glowered, stepping forward. The local men parted in his wake. Reggie had a long fuse, a gentle goliath by nature, but when riled, was a force to be reckoned with. The locals had seen him break up a fight or two at the pub and wanted no part of this.

The fat man looked into Betty's eyes, and then into the enraged giant of a man's face. It was a no-win situation. He raised his hands in the air in supplication and backed off.

"All of you get back to whatever you were doing before you turned into a mob," Betty commanded. "Any more nonsense and I'll arrest each and every one of you."

"Can you do that, Bets," Reggie whispered in her ear.

"No," she mumbled, "but they don't know that."

The sight of the angry pig, snarling German shepherd, commanding woman, and red-faced titan with hands the size of a grizzly bear's paw, was enough to disperse the crowd.

"What was that all about," Betty asked her father as the people dispersed, heading back to the pub or to the marina in excited groups.

"Gertrude found Brother Twelve's treasure," Morris announced, his raucous head of red hair and long beard in full disarray.

"Say what," Reggie gasped.

"This was lodged in her hoof," Archie said, pulling the coin from his torn pocket and handing it to Betty.

Betty and Reggie examined the gold coin.

"It could be, you know," Reggie murmured. "It's the right year."

"You think it's real," Vi gasped, her voice warbling. The race down to the boat and back had winded her.

"Looks it," Betty replied. "If no one calls to claim it and can prove that they own it, then I'll get hold of Tom Powder. It's not something I want to keep around the house for long, not with the way that mob was acting."

"If that there is a piece of Brother Twelve's treasure, then there must be more," Morris noted with noticeable glee.

"If it is, we're in real trouble, Bets," Reggie warned her.

"Why?"

"Treasure hunters," Vi said, agreeing with Reggie. "It's already all over the internet. I bet Gertie will be back on the evening news tonight."

"Damn social media," Betty moaned. "It's only one coin. It doesn't mean there are more."

"That may be, but it won't stop the low-life's from heading here in droves," Archie added.

"Ruddy Hell," Betty groaned. "I've got a couple of calls to answer right now. Sadie Stewart called me. She thinks there's someone in her sister's house."

"What's the other one," Vi asked.

"Oh, some idiot flashed Pearl Tullis."

Archie, Violet, and Morris broke out laughing.

"How did she know," Archie chortled. "She's blind as a bat."

"Heard him unzip and zip up his fly," Betty chuckled. "Pearl found it amusing, but I don't. The kids are all home for the summer. What if he flashes a little girl?"

"I'll go check on Pearl if you want, Betty," Morris offered. "It's on my way home. I'm not going back to the pub, not with that lot in there."

"Oh dear, with all the excitement, I forgot. Our burgers will be cold, Archie," Vi moaned.

"We can warm them up," Archie replied. "Go ask Stew to pack them up for us while I get Gertrude home and check on Peaches."

"That's a good idea, Dad. Morris, I would appreciate it if you would stop in to see Pearl. Tell her I'll be by later. Reg and I are going to go over to Tempe's house and check it out."

"I'd prefer if you keep that coin too, angel puss," Archie said to his daughter. "It gives me the willies just looking at it and I don't want to be responsible for it."

"I will, Pops," Betty agreed.

"Who's a good dog," Reggie murmured, rubbing the German shepherd's head. "You did a great job, buddy."

The dog wagged its tail and all but grinned at Reggie.

Archie started tugging Gertrude by the ear. It didn't take much to get her to start walking home beside him. Peaches was long gone.

Betty and Reggie waited for Vi to return with Vi's and Archie's lunch. She wasn't going to let Vi or her father walk home without making sure they weren't followed.

The crowd gathering on the pub's patio was getting larger by the minute.

"Maybe we should go back to Desolation Sound," Reggie offered.

"Wouldn't that be nice," she said wistfully, "but I think I better call Tom Powder sooner rather than later. We might need the RCMP's help to keep a lid on this."

"You think it will get that bad?"

"People have killed for a lot less than the thought of finding the Sorcerer's gold. I don't want my pig and my father caught in the crossfire."

"Yer right," Reggie said, turning quickly as a ruckus erupted on the porch steps when Vi tried to leave with two doggie bags to go.

"I'll deal with this," the old fisherman hissed.

Reggie strode across the landing looking every bit a Viking King.

Vi looked up into the angry face of the same fat man who threatened Betty's father and animals accosted the tiny woman. She was a feisty old woman and wouldn't back down, no matter how close the man got to her. Forty years on the bench as a family law judge had taught her never to back down, never to doubt her judgement, and never show to show fear or emotions in a courtroom.

Reggie leapt up the pub's steps two at a time.

The fat man scowled and backed away from the tiny wizened judge.

Reggie glared down at him and politely offered Violet his arm. Violet wrapped her dainty arm under his and everyone stepped aside as Reggie escorted her down the pub's steps.

The fat man fled inside the pub, a look of pure malice on his face.

Tempest in a Tea Pot

Sadie unlocked the house and pushed open the door, moving aside so that Betty could enter.

"Can you wait outside and hold on to Champ," she asked Reggie.

"Ya sure ya don't want Champ and me to come in," Reggie replied, his bushy white eyebrows rising. "Champ will be able to tell ya right away if'n anybody's there. That sniffer of his should be registered as a lethal weapon."

"He's certainly a beautiful dog," Sadie cooed, fussing over the German shepherd.

The dog woofed and lapped up the attention.

"I'll call if I need back-up," Betty advised Reggie.

Betty entered the house, her sandals squeaking on the cream-colored marble floors. The house was a monstrosity in her estimation. Who needed this much space?

"Hello," she called, her voice echoing in the grand foyer.

The house was as silent as a morgue.

Betty walked through the downstairs family and living rooms, and then proceeded to the kitchen. The counters were spotlessly clean, but there was a single white china plate, a grey hand pottered mug, and a fork and knife in the sink. She felt the dishes and cutlery: they were all dry.

Betty returned to the foyer where Sadie was anxiously waiting alongside a placid Reggie and the sleepy guard dog.

"Were there dishes in the sink when you were here a couple of hours ago?"

"I didn't notice any," Sadie answered, "but I got spooked by the noises upstairs so I can't be sure. I checked the fridge yesterday and was surprised to find a fresh carton of milk. Tempe is meticulous about leaving food that might rot when she goes away and brought me over some fruit and veggies when she left. I think I remember her dropping off a small carton of milk too, but my kids go through so much milk we were thinking of getting a cow like Peaches."

Reggie and Betty chuckled.

"Okay, I'm going to check upstairs now," Betty responded.

Betty wasn't expecting any trouble. It probably was racoons on the roof, or maybe a squirrel got in the attic. Every house had its own sound and this home was so vast that it was cavernous. Even a little sound could sound big.

Betty climbed the oak stairs, half expecting to see Granny chasing Ellie May down the banister. She had loved the Beverley Hillbillies classic TV show as a kid.

Betty checked each of the three bedrooms, opening closets and peering inside to see if anything appeared disturbed, but nothing seemed out of place. She then strolled into the Master bedroom.

Betty giggled when she saw the enormous four poster king sized bed. Reggie would love it. His feet wouldn't stick out the end of this one.

She checked the bathroom. The towels were dry and there were no water stains in the claw foot tub or the separate shower.

Betty returned to the bedroom and walked quietly around the room. The bed was made, the corners squared to perfection, sheets and blankets tucked in tight.

If someone had been in the house, then they were gone now. The whole place had a feeling of 'emptiness'; it was as much a spiritual void as anything else.

Betty didn't know Tempest Stewart that well. She had heard rumors that she was a bit of a prima donna. Tempe was the exact opposite of her sister, Sadie, who everyone loved and adored.

Betty exited the upstairs and returned to the front entrance.

"There's no one here. No noises. Nothing seems out of place," she advised Sadie.

"Maybe I was just spooked," Sadie confessed. "It's such a big house. Sam out did himself when he built it for Tempest. It almost bankrupted him. It scared me being in it alone. Maybe I transmitted my fear to Cindy. She was growling up a storm which made me think someone was upstairs."

"I guess Sam was planning on a large family when he built the house," Reggie offered.

"Yeah, he did," Sadie agreed. "He hated being an old child."

"Divorce is tough," Betty said as she watched Sadie lock the house back up. "He wouldn't still have a key, would he? Sam, I mean."

"I don't think so. Last I heard, he had moved to Alberta and was working for an outfit there. I feel silly calling you like this," the young woman blushed.

"Naw, don't feel that ways," Reggie guffawed. "We don't mind helping ya out when yer hubby's not here, do we, Bets?"

"We don't indeed," Betty agreed. "If you hear any noises again or see any lights go on that shouldn't be on, then you call me immediately. We'll come down and I'll check the house again."

"Aye, there're a lot of strangers on the island right now with tourist season in full swing and it's better ta be safe than sorry," Reggie responded.

"Thank you both," Sadie gushed, "and you too, Champ."

The dog yawned and wagged his tail.

They walked together down the drive until Sadie left to chase after her son who was racing down the hill behind their property on a bike not designed for mountain trails.

"You think someone was in the house," Reggie asked Betty as they strolled hand in hand back to Betty's house, the German shepherd trotting along beside them, his tail wagging.

"Not that I can see," Betty replied softly, "but the dishes in the sink may indicate otherwise, but without being able to ask Tempe about it, I think we'll just have to wait to hear back from Sadie if she hears or notices anything else."

"Hmmm," Reggie mumbled.

The sun was slowly dropping towards the west and a light breeze rustled the alder and willow bushes that bordered the road. The sky was starting to cloud over. The air felt charged as if a storm was brewing.

"Are you going to spend the night at home or my place," she queried lightly.

"I should go home," he grumbled. "I've left the kids to their own devices long enough. I need to check on the greenhouses and send in a report to the company."

"They aren't really kids, you know," Betty laughed.

"They are to me," Reggie grinned.

They reached the end of Betty's driveway. Her Cape Cod home was directly across the road from her father's cottage, but Betty's house wasn't visible from the road.

"You know I still don't know if I like ya living here," Reggie murmured. He stopped and stared absently into the forest that lined her drive.

"Why," she gasped, shocked.

"Jumping Jiminy, Bets, Andy almost killed yer pa and Vi," Reggie said, rubbing a gnarled hand through his beard. "If it wasn't fer Gertie, they'd be dead, and maybe you too, but then he goes and leaves ya his house in his will. It just never made any sense to me, is all."

"I didn't realize it bothered you so much," she offered, leaning forward for a quick kiss.

Reggie held the kiss longer than she expected.

"I know Andy was sick. We know that fer sure. What we don't know and probably never will is if he killed Eliza," Reggie said, his face creasing with worry. "And ya knows I love yer, but maybe ya should think of selling this place. I just don't think it's right that ya should live here.

We don't know if it was only Barney's moonshine that drove Andy crazy."

Betty stood there, arms wrapped around Reggie's waist, a smile tickling her lips as Reggie looked everywhere but into her eyes.

Was this his way of asking her to move in with him?

Was she ready to even consider it?

Betty loved him, enjoyed his company, but wasn't sure she wanted to go any further than this – not yet at any rate.

Betty had never imagined owning a home like she had now, not after living in Vancouver for so many years. The price of a single-family home was more than her salary could manage, and her pension couldn't support owning a house either.

She loved Seal Island. When she was young, she couldn't wait to leave. Now, at fifty-three, she couldn't imagine living anywhere else.

Betty laughed lightly as she brushed a strand of grey curly hair from Reggie's face.

"What's so funny," Reggie purred into her ear, a great rumble that made Betty's heart flutter.

Betty looked up into Reggie's steel grey eyes, tanned face, and four-day old scruff of a beard. The love that shone down upon her was as bright as a solar flare.

"I was thinking about how lucky I am," she whispered, the words catching in her throat.

The dog wiggled his way in between them.

The two laughed.

"You hold onto that thought and I'll see you tomorrow," Reggie beamed.

"I'll do that," she said, breaking away from him. "Come on, Champ, let's go home. I think a nap is in order, then we'll go visit Pearl and fetch Gertrude and Peaches home from Dad's."

"Don't forget to take that coin out of your pocket and put it in the safe," Reggie advised her.

"Ooh, thanks, honey, I forgot about that," she said, pulling out the gold coin. "I'll call Tom Powder in Vancouver later too."

Reggie waved good-bye and then strolled down the road, heading for home. Who'd have ever thought that the pot smuggler who she had helped secure a medical growing permit instead of busting him every time she came home to visit would end up a millionaire after selling the rights to his unique lines of cannabis for a cool five million plus a percentage of the profits. Looking at him in his holey jeans, discolored Adidas, oil smudged t-shirt and worn ball cap, no one could ever imagine that he was not just a millionaire but a man on the cutting edge of medicinal cannabis development.

Betty grinned as she watched him go. Reggie had changed. He was no longer the pot smuggling fisherman who blushed three shades of red and stammered uncontrollably whenever he looked at her.

Betty ambled up the road to her pretty two storey gabled house, contemplating the double eagle gold coin in her hand. Her serene thoughts disintegrated into a maelstrom of dark emotions. Her smile disappeared and lines of worry replaced the light heartedness she had felt while wrapped in Reggie's arms.

There was a storm coming to Seal Island and the thought terrified her.

As if in agreement, the island trembled as a crack of thunder shook the earth.

***

Morris Tweedsmuir walked up South Shore Road at a ground eating pace. He had told Betty that he would stop in to check on Pearl Tullis, which he would in time, but he was more interested in following the pot-bellied pig and the cow's tracks in the dusty gravel.

The key to finding the treasure was in following the tracks back to where the illustrious pig and cow had been.

He knew he didn't have a lot of time. Someone else was bound to realize that backtracking the pig and cow could net them a fortune. Finders keepers as they say, and Morris intended that he be the one to find the lost treasure.

What would he do with a million dollars or more if the estimates of what Brother Twelve's gold coins were worth was true? The last he heard was that they could be worth at least six million dollars.

Thunder peeled. Lightning flashed. The first drops of rain spattered like meteors hitting the dry dusty ground.

"Oh, no. No. No, no, nooooo," Morris wailed.

"Damnable rain," a hoarse baritone barked behind him.

Morris turned to see Stew Mann, the barrel-chested pub owner, and the stout beer-bellied man who had attacked Archie and threatened Gertrude and Betty's dog, barreling up the road behind him.

"Stew, what are ya doing here," Morris asked, unable to hide the surprise in his voice.

"No different than you, I expect," the fat man growled.

"Easy now, Pete, Morris is a friend of mine," Stew cautioned his brother.

The rain started falling harder. It bounced off the gravel packed road, quickly obliterating the pig and cow's dusty imprints.

"I was going to check on Pearl Tullis," Morris half-lied.

"Hah, you were following the pig's trail," Stew's brother glowered.

"That ain't true," Morris fidgeted.

"Doesn't matter anyway, the rain's destroying the tracks," Stew exclaimed, a note of resignation in his voice.

"And who is this Pearl Tullis," the fat man asked angrily.

"Leave it alone, Pete, we're all too late," Stew replied. "Morris, this is my brother, Pete."

"I can see the resemblance," Morris stuttered, ducking under the limbs of a tall maple tree as the skies opened and a sheet of rain hammered the ground.

Stew and Pete Mann jogged beneath the tree. They huddled under the foliage, the rain falling so hard that it stung when it hit bare flesh. The men stood still, brows knit together, jaws taut with tension.

"So why are you going to see Pearl, Morris," Stew asked good-naturedly.

"Oh, she called Betty. Some fella flashed her. Can you imagine?"

Stew started laughing. It broke the tension.

"What's so funny," Pete Mann grumbled.

"Pearl is waiting for cataract surgery. She can barely see shadows. My wife used to check on her regularly," Stew said, falling silent. He had just filed for divorce. His wife was in jail for first degree murder and attempted murder of his bartender.

"Is that right," Pete said, his face flushed, his back rigid.

"Well, it doesn't look like it's going ta let up," Morris stuttered, happy for an excuse to get away from the two brothers.

"No, it doesn't," Stew agreed.

"I'll see ya then, Stew," Morris mumbled. "Nice ta meet ya, er, Pete."

"I'm sure," Pete snorted derisively.

Morris glanced at Stew. Stew appeared lost in thought. Morris shrugged and then bolted out from under the protective cover provided by the maple tree. He ran through the rain, instantly soaked, as the sheets of water drove against him, his sneakers pounding the wet road as he raced towards the safety of Pearl Tullis's little cottage.

Behind Morris the two brothers stood brooding.

***

"So, Mother Nature thwarted us," Pete Mann grumbled.

"That she did," Stew agreed.

"Tell me more about that cop," the fat man said.

"Betty? She's retired, but the RCMP still bring her in on special cases. She's the law around here," Stew answered. "Why?"

"I want to know how big a threat she is," Pete said.

"Now you wait just a minute, big brother. Betty and Archie are friends of mine. Betty's boyfriend, Reggie, and the Judge are too."

"What Judge?"

"Violet Bone, the tiny lady you damned near ran down at the pub."

"She's a Judge?"

"Retired mostly, like Betty, but she still works on the bench when she's needed," Stew replied. "Those two ladies are the toughest broads you'll ever meet. Don't let their age fool you. Betty is one smart cookie and as tenacious as a pit-bull. Reggie Phoenix is her boyfriend."

"That the big man?"

"It is. He's a good man, not the sharpest tool in the shed unless it comes to growing pot or navigating the islands around here, but he's smart enough to not get caught smuggling dope for twenty years."

Pete considered his options. Right now, there weren't many.

"I'm warning you, you mess with that pig or cow again, and you'll have the whole island to deal with. Folks damn near killed a cop after he tasered the cow when he meant to hit the pig," Stew cautioned his brother.

Pete guffawed.

"It's the truth. You threaten to kill that pig again and it's you who'll be in the fry pan," Stew cautioned him.

"What's at the end of this road," Pete asked, changing the subject.

"Nothing but trees, brush, and ocean," Stew answered. "And if you think you want to go exploring it, watch out for the wild sheep. The rams are dangerous this time of year."

Pete howled with laughter…now there were wild sheep too. This was quite the place. He wondered what made his brother choose Seal Island as the place to settle down on.

Thunder boomed.

A blinding whip of lightning lit up the sky.

Pete noticed his brother had started to shiver. He had gotten soft. Pete knew his brother's ex-wives had cleaned him out and he was just barely holding on to the pub. Stew needed the money. Pete wanted it.

"How much did you owe Betty Bruce compared to me? Blood is blood after all," Pete casually asked his brother, pulling a stub of a cigar from his pocket and lighting up. They weren't going anywhere soon.

"What do you mean by that," Stew whined.

"I mean," Pete said, and then took a drag on the cigar. "Can I trust you to back me up in a crunch."

Stew blanched.

Pete suspected he had his answer.

Things That Go Bump in the Night

Sadie scooted the kids off to bed and opened the back door for their old tomcat and her Yorkie to go outside to do their business. She followed them outside. The Yorkie always required a watchful eye; it was the perfect size for a racoon, owl or eagle to carry off.

The sunset was still a glow with deep reds, pinks and purples on the western horizon. Overhead the stars were already twinkling, and a half moon was rising. The air was warm and breezy.

The summer storm had blown through quickly. She had been surprised at its ferocity. The rain had come down in sheets. The thunder and lightning had terrified her little girl and the small dog. Her son, as usual, had wanted to stand in the rain and watch the lightning. She didn't blame him. She would have too if it wasn't for her peeing dog and wailing child.

Sadie leaned against the back-porch railing. She wore short cut-offs and a tank top. Frogs croaked and crickets chirped. The air smelled fresh and clean. The sweet scent of fir mingled with the harsher scent of cedar. Bats flitted about, catching their fill of bugs, and then flying off in a swarm, disappearing into the dark forest.

Her tom cat's eyes glowed green in the dark, its tail twitching as it lifted its nose to the air, whiskers a quiver. It then strode off into the twilight as if it were a lion leading its pride on an evening hunt.

Suddenly, Cindy, her tiny little Yorkie, yipped and raced off.

"Cindy, come back," Sadie yelled, startled.

Sadie grabbed a flashlight from a side table beside the door and ran after her little dog.

The dog's sharp yip echoed in the dark.

An owl hooted.

Terror gripped Sadie as she imagined the owl swooping down, its talons sinking into her tiny Yorkie's flesh.

"Cindy, stop," she hollered, the flashlight's beam bouncing over the ground in front of her as she pursued the dog.

The young dark-haired woman ran through a series of berry bushes, scratching her arms and legs as she did so. She emerged onto the small track that wound its way around the back of her sister's property.

"Cindy," she called again, reducing her pace.

Sadie heard a growl. She swung the light around. Two raccoons the size of a Cocker spaniel stared back at her, their yellow eyes glittering like highway markers in the flashlight's beam. They chittered a warning as two cubs poked their heads out of the salal bush behind them.

That's all she needed. Raccoons had killed their last cat, a tiny little Siamese that had been no match for the hungry critters. The Yorkie was half the size of that cat.

Sadie spun back around, tears in her eyes, and tripped. She fell flat on the ground, the wind knocked out of her, the flashlight flying into the tall grass beside the little trail.

The Yorkie jumped into her lap as the woman sat up.

"Cindy, thank goodness," she cried, hugging the trembling dog. "What were you thinking, you naughty girl."

Sadie wiped the dirt from her hands and stood up, cradling the dog in one hand.

She bent down to pick up the flashlight and caught a flash of movement inside the upper bedroom window of her sister's house.

"I knew someone was in the house," she whispered to the dog.

She waited a moment, but nothing further happened.

She bit her lip.

Should she call Betty? What if it was another false alarm?

"I'm taking you home first, and then I'm going over there," the nervous woman told the dog.

Sadie picked her way along the back of her sister's and her property until she reached her own home. She grabbed the gold key off the key ring by the door, locked her little dog inside her house, and then marched back over to her sister's place.

Her hands shook as she unlocked the front door.

She pushed it open and flipped on the foyer light.

The empty house was silent.

"You're losing it," Sadie muttered to herself.

There was a loud thud from upstairs, followed by a scraping sound and then the tread of footsteps on the ceiling above the foyer. The footsteps grew louder as they moved from west to east over the roof.

"Hey, you, if you don't get out of here right now, I'm calling the cops," Sadie yelled defiantly.

There was a tall umbrella rack by the front door. She grabbed an umbrella and held it out in front of her like a sword. After all, that was what they did in the movies, right?

Sadie crept into the living room. She flicked on the overhead chandelier lights.

The thump came again.

A loud crash followed it.

Sadie yelped in fear.

A cloud of black soot fell from the fireplace, coating the stone mantel and marble floor in a layer of black dust.

"That's it, buster, you're busted. I'm calling the cops," she screamed, backing out of the living room, the chrome tip of the umbrella in her hand flailing about menacingly.

Sadie reached into her pocket to pull out her cell phone.

Her hand came away empty.

She had left it at home.

"Damn it," she muttered, spinning on her heel, and racing out the door.

Behind the fleeing woman, the front door swung wide open, the bright chandelier lights twinkling in the fading twilight.

"Help" came the faint call from the fireplace.

***

Tammy Smith sat on the couch, eating nachos, and watching the world news. Stories of drought, flood, and every calamity under the sun assailed her. Tammy normally didn't watch the news, but Ida Abercrombie, another member of the writer's club, had called her and told her about the gold coin that Gertrude had found. Ida said they had video footage of it on the six o'clock news and Tammy couldn't wait to see it. A recap of the local news should be on any time now.

What a day, Tammy thought as she popped a jalapeno topped nacho into her mouth. First her friend, Pearl, gets flashed and then Betty's pig finds a coin from Brother Twelve's treasure.

Tammy knew more about Brother Twelve than anyone on the island, knew some of his secrets too. Her parents had been part of the original Mandieh Settlement, first at Cedar by the Sea, and later Valdes and DeCourcy Islands. They believed that he was a sorcerer and Tammy did too.

Her mother spoke a lot about Brother Twelve during the few days before she passed. She said that he could rip people's souls right out of their body and was able to predict the future. When he ordered Sarah Tuckett, a retired schoolteacher, to kill herself because she was too old to work, her mother said her father informed her that it was time to leave DeCourcy Island. Tammy's father suspected Brother Twelve of murdering his wife when she delivered him a daughter instead of a son like had been foretold. The birth of his son was supposed to usher in a new world order.

Tammy's father had stolen a small skiff and rowed both he and his wife to Cedar by the Sea where they caught a lift into town with a local farmer. They left DeCourcy Island with nothing but the clothes on their backs.

Tammy's father believed that Brother Twelve was evil incarnate. He told Tammy as much, threatening that Brother Twelve would come and get her if she didn't behave. She had been terrified and wailed for a week afterwards.

Her father said that Brother Twelve had cursed them for leaving The Aquarian Society. Brother Twelve damned anyone who turned their backs on The Great White Lodge of which the Brother, Buddha, Jesus, and Confucius, were all members. Her father blamed all the bad fortune that befell the Smith family after leaving Brother Twelve's compound on the hex that Brother Twelve cast on his disobedient followers, from the death of Tammy's two brothers to the collapse of her father's business in Nanaimo several years later.

The one thing that her father and mother didn't know was how her parent's past would truly come back to haunt them.

Brother Twelve was supposed to have died in Switzerland in 1934. That was what the death certificate said, but Tammy Smith knew different. Like the great Egyptian god of death, Osiris, Brother Twelve, also known as Edward Arthur Wilson and Julian Churton Skottowe, had risen from the dead.

Tammy knew because she had met him.

Tammy's mother had described the prophet to her. He had intense eyes that looked right through you, she said, and a mesmerizing gaze that he used to entrap one's soul. Her mother would cry out in her sleep, swearing that he had visited her in her bedroom and asking Tammy if she didn't smell him. That was the thing her mother said was most alarming about the prophet: he smelled of spice, incense, myrrh, and wet animal.

Brother Twelve did smell, Tammy conceded. He smelled like one of Morris Tweedsmuir's goats and his breath stank of the garlic he was so fond of chewing. He told Tammy that garlic was good for opening one's chakras so that one could more easily receive enlightenment.

There was an aura of power about the Brother that was otherworldly. Sometimes when Tammy sat with him beneath the oak tree that he called the Tree of Knowledge and Truth, he spoke in some strange and exotic language. It was a pretty language, but it involved a lot of spitting.

Tammy believed Edward Arthur Wilson was the twelfth disciple in The Great White Lodge. It was their secret. Tammy was the only person on Seal Island who knew that the quiet hermit living in the sod hut on the beach on the far side of the island was the heretic prophet. He was a very old man then, his hair as white as arctic ice, his beard equally so, his dark brown eyes sunken into his craggy face. Sometimes, there was a tinge of madness in those eyes, and sometimes in his words. As young as she was, she knew to leave him alone during those strange times.

Before Brother Twelve completed his journey in this life, he told Tammy that she would live to see his treasure unearthed by a great bristling boar. Tammy knew where it was buried. He had shown her. Not once in all her years on earth had she revealed its location to anyone. On the day that his treasure was unearthed, Brother Twelve told her that he would come for her, his last true believer.

A commercial filled with skimpily clad girls flashing their pearly white teeth at the camera marketing a new brand of toothpaste blared on the TV. Tammy had no idea what teens in bikinis had to do with toothpaste, but what did she know. After the commercial, the late-night news anchor announced that a gold coin from what was purported to be part of Brother Twelve's treasure had been found on Seal Island.

Tammy leaned forward and put on her glasses so that she could see the screen better. The blue framed readers perched precariously on the end of her nose. She was an old woman after all, but her mind was as clear as the star-spangled sky outside. The video on the screen was shaky, but she could clearly see Gertrude head butt the fat man who tried to snatch the gold coin from Archie Bruce's hand.

Tammy cackled with glee.

She was eighty-five years old and had indeed lived long enough to see the sorcerer's gold unearthed, at least one small piece of it.

There was a loud banging on her front door.

Tammy's brow furrowed. It was too late for anyone to be calling.

"Is that you, Brother," she yelled, pushing herself to her feet. "Have you come for me? Is it my time?"

The thump-thump-thump came again, louder and more urgent this time.

"I'm coming, Brother. I've kept the faith," she yelled.

Tammy walked slowly to the front door, unafraid. She straightened her shoulders as best she could and smoothed down her blouse and summer skirt before opening the door. If it was time to join Brother Twelve in The Great White Lodge, then she wanted to look her best.

She opened the front door, half expecting to see a handsome young Edward Wilson standing there wearing the blue and gold sorcerer's cape that he had pulled from a battered old trunk and draped around her young shoulders. She had felt like a true sorcerer's apprentice beneath it.

Neither Brother Twelve nor anyone she knew stood there. Instead, a young man wearing a black leather duster like Clint Eastwood wore in his Western movies, a crisp white shirt, and a black top hat greeted her.

As he unzipped his fly, Tammy Smith burst into a gale of laughter so loud and so consuming that her heart burst. She dropped dead in her doorway, taking the secrets of Brother Twelve with her.

Knock Three Times

Betty was sitting on the back-porch sipping on a glass of red wine watching the dying rays of the sunset, contemplating the day's events. Champ was curled up on the mat by her feet. She had brought Gertrude and Peaches home from her father's and they were now safe in their stalls in the barn.

Betty's cell phone buzzed.

She glanced at the face: 'private caller' was all it said.

"Hello," she said, answering the call.

"Betty, it's Sadie again," Sadie's voice boomed over the cell's speaker.

"What's happened," Betty asked, putting her glass down on the table beside her.

"There's definitely someone in the house. I heard footsteps," the young woman gushed excitedly, "and then a loud thump."

"I'm on my way," Betty said, hanging up the phone.

"Come on, Champ, police dog mode," she barked, nudging the dog awake.

The dog yawned and stretched.

"Don't look so excited," she chuckled.

Betty thought about calling Reggie and asking him to meet her at Sadie's, but Reggie didn't own a vehicle and his property was on the far side of South Shore Road. Sadie's house was either a fifteen-minute walk from Betty's home or a two-minute drive. Betty's Jeep could use a run, so she decided to drive.

Betty grabbed the car keys from the house and strode quickly to the barn. The dog trotted eagerly beside her, sensing the urgency in Betty's long stride.

Betty checked briefly on the sleeping pig and cow, closing and bolting Gertrude's stall door as she did so. The dog whined.

"No Gertie for back-up this time, Champ," she told the dog.

Betty opened the rear passenger door of her Jeep. The shepherd jumped in. She ran around the front of the vehicle and slipped into the driver's seat.

It was less than five minutes from Sadie's frantic phone call to Betty's arrival at Tempest Stewart's house. The door to the house stood wide open. Sadie was nowhere in sight.

Betty let the dog out of the car.

"Heel," she commanded the German shepherd.

The dog leaned into her, heeling so close that she almost tripped over it as she jogged up the front steps.

"Police," she yelled out of habit. She reached for a sidearm, swearing lightly when the realization hit for the twentieth time that she didn't carry one anymore.

Not for the first time, Betty wondered if she shouldn't start packing a gun on calls like this anyway. Armed back-up was a ferry or helicopter ride away. A dog and a pot-bellied pig weren't always enough.

"Heeellllp," a masculine voice called out.

Betty followed the voice into the living room. She looked around, puzzled.

"Where are you," Betty hollered back.

"In here," the man gasped. His voice was weak and strained.

Betty was truly puzzled. The dog hugged her left leg.

"Search, Champ," she commanded the dog.

Champ whined and ran straight to the fireplace. He looked her in the eye and sat down.

"Seriously," Betty said to the dog.

The dog barked, stood up, and then sat down again, nose pointing towards the fireplace.

Betty kneeled and looked up the chimney. She saw two sneaker clad feet and pajama covered legs.

"How the devil did you get in there," Betty asked the trapped man.

"Fell down the chimney when I was adjusting the satellite dish," the man hissed.

"Sam, is that you?"

"Yeah."

"Is that pajamas you're wearing?"

"Yeah."

"Why?"

"I've been living in the attic."

Betty smothered a giggle. It really wasn't funny, but she couldn't help herself.

"I know you're laughing," he grumbled.

"I thought you were working in Alberta," she said, rubbing the dog's ears.

"I got laid off," was his answer.

"Betty! Who is it," a wide-eyed Sadie asked, creeping into the house. Her son's baseball bat replaced the black umbrella. She held the aluminum bat out in front of her, ready for anything.

"It's your former brother-in-law," Betty responded.

"Sam? What is he doing here," she blurted out, puzzled? She glanced around. There was no one in the room but Betty and her dog. "Where is he?"

"Stuck in the chimney," Betty snorted, unsuccessfully covering her amusement.

"Hi, Sadie," Sam mumbled from inside the chimney.

"Oh my gosh, Sam," Sadie cried out, dropping the bat. It clattered loudly as it rolled across the tile floor.

Sadie rushed over to the fireplace, and then stared up the chimney. "Why are you in pajamas?"

"He's been living in the attic," Betty responded. "That's what the thumping you heard was. Probably why there were dishes in the sink too."

"Hey, I cleaned up after myself," he muttered angrily. "Can someone please get me out of here? It's getting hard to breathe."

"I'll call the volunteer fire department," Betty said, pulling out her phone.

"Seriously, Sam, why are you HERE?"

"I had nowhere else to go," the broken man sobbed. "I knew Tempe was gone. She sent me a frigging text message telling me she had finally met her soul mate."

"I know, she can be a real gnat sometimes," Sadie consoled the trapped man.

"Sometimes?"

Betty walked across the room and called the fire chief. She spoke quietly into the phone as she summoned the members of the volunteer fire department. Her dog sat beside Sadie on the fireplace mantel, looking up at the dangling sneakers and blue and green plaid pajama bottoms worn by the man inside the chimney as if these two things were the most fascinating items in all the world. Betty doubted that even a strip loin steak dangled in front of Champ's nose would break his gaze for very long.

It took some time for the laughter to die out on the other end of the call as the fire chief assured her that they would be there quickly.

"The fire department will be here in about fifteen to twenty minutes," Betty said, ambling back across the room. There was no need to hurry. Sam wasn't going anywhere.

"You know, Sam, you could have called me. You could have stayed with us. You're still my kids' favorite uncle," Sadie said. "I don't care what my sister might have to say about it."

"Thanks, Sadie, maybe when I get out of jail."

"You might not go to jail," Betty replied, hunkering down by the fireplace. "It depends on if Tempe presses charges."

Betty's statement was met with silence.

Sadie looked at the older woman and shrugged. With a sinking feeling, Betty realized that given Tempest's nature, charges would be pressed.

Betty's phone buzzed again. She looked at the phone's ID. It was another 'Private Caller'.

"Excuse me," she said, leaving Sadie to console her ex-brother-in-law.

Betty walked out onto the front porch and answered the call.

"Is this Betty," an old woman's voice asked.

"It is," Betty replied, not quite able to place the voice.

"This is Pearl Tullis," the woman said. "I hate to bother you, but it's a little late to ask Ida to go see if Tammy is okay. I know this sounds strange, but I have the feeling that something has happened to her."

Betty had learned to trust her gut feelings over the years and never doubted someone else when they told her about theirs.

"It's no trouble, Pearl. I had meant to stop and see you today, but time kind of slipped away on me."

"I heard about the ruckus at the pub," Pearl said. "Is it true that Gertrude found a gold coin belonging to Brother Twelve?"

"She found a coin. Whether it was Brother Twelve's or not remains to be proven."

"Oh, dear," Pearl groaned. "That's going to be nasty. I'm glad we've got you on the case."

Betty smiled.

"Thank you, Pearl," she replied. "I'm out on another call. I'm probably going to be awhile yet, but I'll swing by Tammy's house and check in on her. I'll stop by and see you tomorrow."

"Do phone me or have Tammy phone me tonight to let me know that she's okay," the woman pleaded. "She'd do that for me."

"I will," Betty promised, hanging up the phone.

It was a good thing she had just enjoyed five days out on the boat with Reggie. It looked like she was going to have a couple of busy days ahead of her. It was getting to the point that Seal Island needed a full-time police officer. She was supposed to be retired. So much for that.

An hour later, the island's sole fire truck pulled in. The fire chief and several of the island's volunteer firefighters jumped out, all of them dressed in full firefighting gear.

Betty thought it was a good thing this wasn't a fire. She supposed they had to get their giggles out before they arrived.

"How's Sam doing," the chief asked as his men trod through the house, silly grins on their faces.

"Okay, but he says it's getting hard for him to breathe in there," Betty replied.

Betty followed the fire chief back into the living room.

"How on earth are we going to get him out," one of the firefighter's asked.

"Any suggestions, Sam," Sadie yelled up the chimney. "You built the house."

"You're gonna have to cut through the drywall and the bricks," Sam called in return. His voice was hoarse, both from the tight quarters and embarrassment.

"Yep," the fire chief agreed, staring up the brick chimney at Sam's sneakers. "You did a good job on this chimney, Sam."

"Thanks," Sam grumbled.

"Looks like you broke the flume coming down," the chief said.

"Expect so," was the garbled response.

"Okay, you men go get the saws," the chief ordered. "And maybe some sledgehammers and axes too."

Betty shook her head as she watched the firefighters head back to the fire truck, a jaunt in their step, eyes crinkling with mirth. There was nothing like the idea of half demolishing a house with axes, chainsaws, and hammers, to bring a smile to a man's face. The dog followed them, its tail wagging furiously. It was a toss-up as to who was having the most fun.

"Chief, I have another call to make," Betty said, pulling the fire chief aside.

"What's up, Bets," he asked. "Is this anything to do with Brother Twelve's treasure?"

"No," she snorted mirthlessly. "Pearl Tullis called me. She asked me to go check on Tammy Smith. Pearl's just worried about her, is all."

"You want one of my men to go with you," he asked. "I heard about the flasher. Must be a tourist. Can't imagine one of our folks doing that."

"I'll be fine. Thanks for offering," she said.

***

Betty left the craziness behind her. She drove slowly down North Shore Road, past the busy pub, the over-flowing marina, and the small boardwalk that joined the pub and the general store together. A couple dozen white artisan tents, empty now, dotted the lawn between the boardwalk and the beach where local farmers sold their products alongside potters, wood workers, and jewelers during daylight hours.

She turned left on South Shore Road, the half-moon in the sky lighting her way almost as much as the headlights on her new Jeep Wrangler. The tall fir and cedar trees that bordered the road on either side were as dark and foreboding as Sleepy Hollow. Misty shrouds twined through the base of the trees like wraiths.

Betty shivered as she slowed to a stop on the road in front of Reggie's cottage. The glow from the four long greenhouses at the back of his property was blinding.

She gnawed on her lower lip. Reggie was probably sleeping. It was later than she expected. Did she really need to bother him for this small an errand?

The dog voiced its disapproval when she pulled away.

Betty continued up the winding road. A small herd of deer grazed by the side of the road. She had to stop a couple of times, both for deer and to let a herd of feral sheep cross the road. The sheep were a bane to local environmentalists, but she liked them and prayed they were never rounded up.

Betty parked in front of Tammy Smith's old homestead. The lights were on in all the windows. Betty felt her heart sink as she stepped out of the Jeep. Just like at Tempe Stewart's house, the front door was wide open.

"Champ, heel," she said, opening the rear door for the dog.

The dog instantly started to growl, a low rumble that built in fierceness as Betty pushed open the garden gate and strode purposefully towards the front door.

"Tammy," she gasped, seeing the body lying on the ground just outside the doorstep.

"Champ, sit," she instantly ordered the dog. "Stay."

The dog continued to rumble deep within its chest but stayed where commanded.

Betty rushed over to check for a pulse but wasn't expecting one. Tammy's face was already pale and slack in death. Her eyes were starting to glaze over, a sure sign that the old woman had been dead for some time.

"At least it wasn't Gertrude this time," she sighed. Her pig had a penchant for finding bodies.

Betty dialed the local Vancouver Island RCMP Detachment. She walked through the house as she spoke to the Detachment's duty officer. She noticed the congealing pile of nachos on the table. Other than that, there were no signs of a struggle. She instinctively turned off the blaring television as she walked by it. Whatever, or whoever, had brought Tammy to the door was long gone.

"Looks like a heart attack," Betty advised the duty sergeant. "There's no blood and no signs of a disturbance anywhere. A friend of hers called me and asked me to check in on her."

Betty listened as the duty sergeant asked a few more questions.

"Tammy Smith is her name. She's somewhere around eighty-five or eighty-six, maybe older. I'm not completely sure. Her family was one of the original settlers on the island," Betty replied.

Betty went to the linen closet and pulled down a clean sheet. She returned to the front entry and placed the sheet over Tammy's body.

"I've left the body intact but have covered it," she advised the duty officer.

"You'll come tonight? Okay, I'll wait for your arrival. Tell the ambulance and officers to turn right when they come off the barge. It's the second last house on South Shore Road. My Jeep is parked outside the gate."

Betty listened for a moment and then hung up the phone. She stepped over Tammy's body, a sharp tinge of regret and pain making her chest tight. She dreaded the call to Pearl. She and Tammy had been life-long friends. As far as Betty knew, Tammy had no family to notify. She had never married and never had children.

The thought brought her to tears.

She bent down and hugged her dog.

After a couple of minutes, she stood up and returned to the Jeep, prepared to hunker down for a couple of hours. It would take that long at least for the ambulance and police to get to the island, unless they decided to fly in. The barge operator wasn't always willing to do an extra run at night.

Betty realized that she hadn't mentioned Sam to the desk sergeant, nor had she made a call to Inspector Tom Powder about the coin that Gertrude had found. Sam may or may not need medical attention after the fire department freed him from the chimney. As far as his arrest for trespass and property destruction, she'd leave that for Tempest and her new husband to decide when they returned from their cruise.

The coin was another matter.

Suddenly, the thought of the stick thin, bleached blond pinch faced Barbie doll, Tempest Stewart, returning to the destruction in the living room turned the tears of sorrow in Betty's eyes into ones of laughter.

Betty hammered the steering wheel with her fists, laughing uncontrollably.

Champ licked her face.

Betty pushed him away, trying valiantly to regain her composure.

Just as the laughing slowed, Betty realized that she didn't even know the name of the man the high maintenance young girl had just married. Surely, he wasn't a local. The local boys knew better.

Betty burst into another fit of giggles.

Champ woofed loudly and wagged his tail, joining in the fun.

Betty's cell phone buzzed. She looked at the display. It was the fire chief.

"You want the good news or the bad news first," he asked after she answered the call.

"What's the good news," she replied, wiping the tears from her eyes.

"Sam is okay. He looks like a lost puppy whose been hiding under the woodshed for a week, but he'll be fine. Sadie took him home."

"So, what's the bad news," Betty queried, picturing the crew of delighted firefighters walking through the house carrying axes, chainsaws, and the biggest hammers she had ever seen.

"As we were packing up to leave, one of the fellows noticed smoke billowing out of the attic," the chief said, pausing for effect.

"Oh my God," Betty hissed.

"Karma's a bitch isn't it," he chuckled.

Betty snorted in amusement.

"The boys are working on it now. I just thought I'd give you a call. You may want to stop by for smores," the chief joked.

"Thanks, I'll pass," Betty replied, her grin disappearing. "Tammy Smith has passed away. Looks like a heart attack. I'm waiting for the police and ambulance. It'll probably be a couple of hours before they get here."

"Oh, no, I liked that old girl. There aren't many of the original residents left anymore," he said, his own humor disappearing.

"Don't let any of your crew know. I want to tell Pearl myself before anyone else has a chance."

"Will do, Bets," he said, using Betty's nickname. "Give her a hug from me too."

Betty hung up, wondering if the night would ever end.

"Champ, I need you to watch over Tammy while I go see Pearl," she told the dog. "Don't let any critters get to her."

Betty opened her door and then let the dog out. Pearl's ramshackle house was a twenty-minute walk down the road and right now she needed the fresh air to calm her nerves. She also didn't want Pearl to find out her friend had died the hard way: a cavalcade of police cars and an ambulance rolling by her home at midnight or a call from someone at the pub after the firefighters descended upon it once the flames at the *Gone with the Wind* mansion were extinquished.

The Emancipation of Tammy Smith

Pearl's house was lit up like a lighthouse on a stormy night. Every light was on including the outside porch lights. Betty wasn't surprised. With Pearl's fading eyesight it made sense.

Betty looked through the living room window as she walked up the path leading to the front door. She could see Pearl sitting in front of the TV. The volume was turned up so loud she could hear what type of show Pearl was watching: *America's Got Talent*. Betty grinned. She liked that show too.

The inside metal door was open, leaving the screen door to guard against the mosquitoes and moths that buzzed about. Several large white and grey moths circled the porch light.

Betty knocked loudly. There was no answer. It wasn't a surprise given how loud the TV was. She knocked again and then pulled on the screen door's handle.

"Pearl, it's Betty," she yelled over the din of the television.

"What," Pearl cried, lowering the volume on the remote.

"It's Betty Bruce," Betty repeated, stepping into the living room.

"Oh, Betty, I'm glad you're here," Pearl said, turning off the TV. "Is Tammy okay?"

Betty pulled a wooden chair across the floor and sat down beside the old woman. She remembered when Pearl's eyes sparkled like blue sapphires. Only a hint of blue was visible now. The intelligent woman was still there though, peeking out from beneath the white glaze of the cataracts that were stealing her vision, slowly like a turtle crossing the road.

"I'm sorry, I have bad news," Betty said, taking one of the woman's gnarled hands in hers. "Tammy's passed away. It looks like a heart attack."

"Nonsense," Pearl cried, tearing up. "She was as strong as a bull."

"Well, we won't know for sure until the coroner files his report, but from what I saw, I believe that's what happened."

Pearl's shoulders trembled.

Betty instinctively wrapped her arms around the woman and let her cry for a few minutes.

"How about I make us a pot of tea," Betty offered.

"That would be lovely," Pearl sniffed. "I still have some of Summer's Mint Medley and that lovely girl, Rainbow, dropped some organic Oolong tea off the other day. I haven't tried it yet."

"Come on then, let's get a cuppa," Betty replied. She was happy that Rainbow had taken an interest in the island's senior residents. She had been worried at first that the island's seniors wouldn't take to the dreadlocked pet psychic, but obviously Betty had been wrong.

Betty helped Pearl to her feet even though the old woman didn't really need it. Pearl was agile for her age. It simply made Betty feel better. She found comfort in the warmth emanating from the old woman's wrinkled calloused hand in hers.

Betty had delivered the news of lost loved ones to so many grief-stricken families during her years on the force that it should have gotten easier, but it never had. The loss of Tammy Smith was personal which made it doubly hard.

The two women walked into the kitchen. Pearl filled the kettle and put it on the stove to boil while Betty searched the cupboards until she found the tea.

"Mint or Oolong," Betty asked.

"Mint, I think," Pearl answered. "It will help calm my nerves."

Betty took down the package of River's Mint Medley tea and then cleaned the teapot while the water began to boil.

Pearl sat down at the kitchen table, her shoulders slumping forward.

"Tammy was a spiritualist. Did you know that?" Pearl queried, more to fill the silence than in expectation of an answer. "She had some very odd views of the world. I always found that strange considering her parents were such fervent church goers. In the old days, the minister came by boat from Nanaimo twice a month, except in the storm season. Mr. Smith conducted the sermons when the minister wasn't here. Tammy's father was all fire and brimstone. He terrified me. I used to beg my mother to let me stay at home. I'd have rather done chores than listen to Mr. Smith's version of Hell. It was too much for my ten-year-old mind to handle."

"I didn't know that."

"Tammy's views were totally opposite of her father's; although, I doubt she ever dared tell him that. They bordered on East Indian and ancient Egyptian for want of a better explanation," Pearl continued. "She believed in the after life, but not like the Bible preaches. She believed in Osiris, the Egyptian God of Death and Fertility, and in the weighing of our souls. She also believed in reincarnation. I expect she will feel quite emancipated when her soul returns from the 'Other Side'."

The white-haired woman smiled sadly.

The kettle whistled.

Betty removed it from the stove and made a pot of tea. She then placed two cups on the table and sat down beside Pearl to wait for the tea to steep.

"Emancipated, as in liberated?"

"Oh, yes," Pearl grinned. "Tammy firmly believed that whether or not we were reborn again was dependent on how much we learned in this life, the good we did, and our strength of belief. She assured me that she had all three and was looking forward to being born again. You aren't planning on having children, are you?"

"Why's that?"

"Because you might end up with Tammy," Pearl chortled lightly. "That's a terrible thought, isn't it?"

"I could do worse," Betty grinned.

"You could," Pearl agreed. "I guess you aren't allowed to wear your red serge anymore, are you? It would be lovely to have you presiding over her funeral like you did at our dear Eliza's."

"I'm afraid not. I still have my dress uniform, but I can't wear it without a letter of approval from the Superintendent."

71

"Pity," Pearl said, pouring the tea.

The sweet scent of camomile, rose hip, and spearmint filled the air. Betty's mouth watered. She instantly felt the tension leave her shoulders.

"You will bring Gertrude and Peaches though, won't you? Tammy loved those two critters. They're such characters. Truth be told, it wasn't just Eliza who liked to have them in for tea. Tammy and I both enjoyed their visits and Gertrude just loved Tammy's shortbreads. I used to make Tammy cut Gertrude off after ten."

"No wonder she's gotten so chunky," Betty laughed.

"Good grief, how can you tell?"

The two women laughed heartily.

"Yes, I'll bring them," Betty agreed.

The women sat in amiable silence for awhile drinking their tea.

"You know," Pearl mused aloud, "it would be funny if Gertrude had babies and Tammy came back as a pot-bellied piglet. I wouldn't put it past her. She'd cause even more havoc than Gertie on this island."

Pearl chuckled.

"Are you sure that Tammy was your friend," Betty asked, a twinkle in her eye.

"Oh, yes, lifelong," Pearl responded, "that's why I can joke about it. I'm quite sure she's listening."

Once again, they sat quietly, each of them lost in their own thoughts and memories. Betty was content to keep Pearl company. She knew how it felt to be alone, your mind conjuring up all sorts of strange images and ideas, after losing someone dear to you.

"You know, Betty, Tammy, Ida and I visited Eliza the morning she died," Pearl said, wandering off track.

"Why didn't one of you ever tell me that," Betty asked, her stomach knotting.

"We didn't think it mattered," Pearl quipped. "Eliza was dead, and Andy had confessed to her murder."

"Pearl," Betty leaned forward, "we don't believe Andy killed anyone. He was high on LSD and had lead poisoning. His confession held no weight. The coroner ruled Eliza's death accidental, but we still aren't absolutely sure of that. Did you see anything?"

Betty grimaced, angry with herself. Of course, Pearl didn't see anything, but maybe Tammy or Ida did. Tammy couldn't comment, but Ida could. She made a mental note to call Ida in the morning.

That raised the question: was Tammy's heart attack accidental? Was Tammy's death linked to Eliza Bone's death? Betty reeled at the implications behind Pearl's casual statement.

"Where on earth did Andy get LSD?"

"Barney's moonshine. He was dosing every other bottle, plus some of his piping was contaminated with lead solder. I thought everyone knew."

"No one told me," Pearl grumbled. "That explains the buzz every time I have a nip of it. Perhaps you better take what's left of the bottle in the cupboard above the stove with you."

"Pearl!"

"What? You think an old lady like me doesn't like a nip of moonshine every so often. I'd have one now if you hadn't mentioned the lead poisoning."

"You mean the idea of dropping LSD doesn't bother you," Betty guffawed.

"Of course not," the old woman confessed. "I'm as emancipated as Tammy."

Betty laughed, the knot in her stomach loosening. After a moment, Pearl joined in.

"At least tell me what you remember about your visit to Eliza's."

"There's not much to tell really. We stopped by for muffins and tea in the morning. We were planning to introduce a new cozy detective series to the club and weren't sure how Tiffany would take it. She was always so focused on her own and Andy's novels. We wanted the Writer's Society to open up the book club part of the writer's society to other authors. That's about it."

"And no one else called or popped by while you were there or when you were leaving," Betty asked.

"Not that I remember. Eliza did say that Archie had been over for a visit before us, but I expect you know that. They were an item, you know," Pearl said conspiratorially.

"Yes, Dad told me."

It had taken Betty's father far too long to tell her about his romance with Eliza. Betty wished that one of the three friends had told her about it. They could have told her that day or after Eliza's funeral service. She couldn't fathom why any one of the dear old souls hadn't been thrilled to impart such news given how much they loved to gossip.

"Did Eliza say anything about feeding her fish," Betty queried. "I know it's a strange question, but I need to ask it given how I found her."

"Oh, she was feeding them when I came out of the loo," Pearl answered.

"What? Are you sure?"

"Definitely. I could see her shadow by the tank. It was taller than usual, so I supposed she was standing on the stool she kept by the fish tank. That darned thing. I walked into it enough. I thanked her for the muffins and told her I'd see her at the next meeting on the way out," Pearl said, her brow furrowing.

"And she didn't say anything back? Nothing at all," Betty asked, a sinking feeling creeping over her.

"No, nothing, but we had already said our good-byes. Anyway, Ida was yelling at me from the back porch to hurry up so off I went," Pearl snorted derisively. "It was a long walk home and I didn't fancy peeing in the bushes along the way. We had already left once, but then I felt nature calling and ran back to the house."

Betty inhaled sharply.

Had Eliza gone to feed her fish after the ladies left, fallen over and bumped her head on the tank while Pearl was in the bathroom or before? If Pearl could see, would she have seen that Eliza was drowning in her own fish tank having been knocked unconscious when Eliza hit her head on the side of the tank? Possibly, yes.

Betty saw the flash of red and white police and ambulance lights on the trees outside the window as the ambulance and three police vehicles cruised by, heading up South Shore Road towards Tammy's house.

"Oh, no, Champ," Betty cried, stumbling as she pushed back her chair and rose too quickly. She hadn't realized she had been there that long.

"Are you alright?"

"Sorry, Pearl, I have to go. The police and ambulance are here."

"Oh, dear, well off you go then," Pearl said. "Thank you for coming. Do pop by again and bring your animals with you – all of them."

"I will," Betty gasped, hurrying out the garden door.

***

Betty jogged after the police cars and ambulance, huffing and puffing with the effort. She had let her training go since she had retired. This was a tough reminder that she needed to start a regimen back up again.

The vehicles came to a halt beside her Jeep. Several RCMP officers stepped out of the cruisers including Sergeant Peter Singh, a friend she hadn't expected to see there. She had heard he had transferred over to a Vancouver detachment.

"Pete, stop," she screamed at the top of her voice. "Champ is there!"

The men didn't hear her.

"STOP," she hollered at the top of her lungs.

Champ's furious barking echoed in the night.

"Champ, sit," Betty yelled, knowing the dog would hear her, if not the police officers. "Break."

The barking instantly stopped.

Betty raced onto the scene.

Singh and two of the officers faced off against the dog, their weapons drawn. The paramedics were running back to the safety of their ambulance.

"I'm guessing that's your dog, Betty," Singh said gruffly, shouldering his weapon, "but I wasn't sure. I thought your dog was timid but this one is all business. Put it away, guys, that's Betty's partner."

"Sorry, Pete," Betty gasped, holding her side as a muscle stitch ripped through it.

Champ sat beside the body, eyes roving from one police officer to the other. He wagged his tail when he saw Betty but didn't leave his post.

"Good dog," Betty said, reaching into her pocket for a dog biscuit. "Heel."

The German shepherd instantly obeyed.

"It's safe to come out," Singh hollered to the ambulance crew.

"I thought you'd gone to the mainland, Pete," Betty said as the two ambulance men wheeled over a gurney.

"My wife didn't want to move to the city, and I didn't either so here I am," he confessed. "Where's Gertrude?"

"She's not on this case," Betty joked. "And you're right, Champ used to be quite the fraidy-cat, but he's come along way since you last saw him. I think he's found his confidence."

The two friends walked over to stand beside the body as an officer carefully removed the sheet that Betty had placed over it. Another officer took photos while another two re-checked the house for any clues as to what brought Tammy outside.

"Definitely looks like a heart attack," a paramedic said, kneeling beside the body. "I don't see any contusions, but the coroner will decide the final cause of death."

Betty nodded having been there before.

"Any idea why she would be in the doorway like that," Pete wondered.

"No idea. I only came to check on Tammy because her friend couldn't reach her and was worried," Betty said.

"Seems pretty cut and dry," Singh concluded. "She may have just been opening the door to let some air in. It's a hot night."

"It sure is," Betty agreed, rubbing Champ behind the ears. The dog panted. It may be a panic attack at all the people around him or because of the heat. Betty didn't know which, but she kept a comforting hand on the dog.

In truth, Champ still suffered from anxiety in crowds despite what she had told Singh, but the shepherd rose to the occasion and followed its commands instead of running away like he used to do in his former job as part of an airport security team. Champ responded better to one owner than several different handlers.

"You remember the night you came to the island after I found Eliza drowned in her fish tank?"

"I do," the sergeant said, pushing a stray lock of black hair back under his turban. "What of it?"

"I just had an interesting chat with Pearl Tullis. She told me that she, Tammy, and another friend, Ida, visited Eliza the morning she died. Since Pearl can't see anything but shadows and Tammy is now dead, I'm going to talk to Ida to see if she remembers anything."

"Think they might shed some more light on it then? Or do you think that Eliza's and this here lady's deaths are linked?"

"I don't know," Betty answered. "I have a feeling that if Ida confirms what Pearl just told me, it will confirm that Eliza's death was indeed a tragic accident and we can close the case once and for all on her death."

"It would be nice for you to find some closure to your friend's death," Pete agreed.

"It would," she agreed. "I can't see the two deaths being related. Right now, I'd like to know what brought Tammy to the door or what gave Tammy such a start that she dropped dead."

"I agree. Keep me posted on your investigations and I'll let you know what the coroner rules," Singh said. "I'll let Head Office know that I've officially invited you onto the case so that you can get paid as a consultant and can have some power behind your inquiries."

"Thanks, Pete."

"I hear you've had a busy night; besides this I mean."

"Yeah, there's a fire on North Shore Road close to my house. The chief told me they have a handle on it."

"You know the cause," Pete asked.

"No idea," Betty said. The half-truth stuck in her throat. The fire chief hadn't told her what caused the fire in the attic although she suspected it had something to do with Sam.

"Well, no one called us so unless the fire chief requests our presence," Pete muttered, raising one eyebrow, "we'll leave it alone."

"Hmmm," Betty agreed. "Have you had any calls about a flasher by chance?"

"No," Singh snorted in amusement. "You have a flasher on the island?"

"We do. He flashed an old lady down the road," she volunteered.

"You think maybe the flasher was here tonight and flashed this old girl? Maybe it triggered the heart attack?"

"Tammy Smith wasn't afraid of anything," Betty guffawed. "Who knows though? Maybe something like that happened. There are tonnes of tourists around this year."

"I noticed," the sergeant agreed. "That marina looked full to capacity."

The ambulance crew and another officer gently placed Tammy's body in a body bag and loaded it onto the gurney.

"I'm exhausted," Betty mumbled. "Just turn off the lights and shut the door behind you once your officers are done. I'll email you a statement in the morning if that is okay?"

"Sure, Bets. Do you know of any next of kin that we should contact?"

"She didn't have any family that I know of, but I'll call Pearl in the morning and phone Ida Abercrombie too. They were close to Tammy. They'll know if she had a Will or if there is anyone you should call."

"That'd be great. Thanks for securing the scene," Singh nodded. "And you too, Champ."

The dog yawned and wagged its tail.

"Let's go buddy," Betty said to the dog. She knew she'd have to stop at Reggie's on the way home as he would have seen the lights and wondered what was going on. After that, she just wanted to go home, finish her glass of wine, and go to bed.

Betty shook her head wearily as she opened the door for Champ to climb into the back of the Jeep. She had forgotten to grab the bottle of moonshine from Pearl. She had also forgotten to mention the gold coin that Gertrude had found to Pete Singh or to call Tom Powder.

She knew she should walk back over to where Pete was standing chatting with his men and tell him about the gold coin, but she didn't. Exhaustion threatened to overwhelm her. Besides, she reasoned, it was better to talk to Tom Powder privately than the sergeant at the scene of an incident.

There was nothing that couldn't wait until morning. The coin was safe in her pocket and Tammy wasn't going to get anymore dead.

Betty closed the back door and sidled into the driver's seat. As she turned the key in the ignition, she contemplated Pearl's words about the emancipation of Tammy Smith. It was an odd way to look at death, but the thought of Betty's deceased friends' souls being reborn, was a thought worth holding onto.

Break and Enter

"I don't like this," Stew growled as he and his brother crept through Betty's house.

"It never used to bother you," his brother retorted.

"That was because I either didn't know the marks or didn't like them," Stew grumbled.

"Fine," Pete snorted with disgust. "Keep a watch out front in case she returns."

Stew mumbled something unintelligible and then descended the stairs to the living room.

Pete continued to rifle through Betty's dresser drawers and bathroom using a small penlight to illuminate the contents in each. He found a gold necklace with a pearl and diamond heart shaped pendant that he pocketed without thinking. Everything else wasn't worth the bother, he groused, practically chastising the woman he was robbing for her frugalness.

He then moved to the study. He switched the desk light on, not as worried about the light being seen since the windows looked over the back of the house.

"And what do we have here," he muttered, finding a small hidden safe inside one of the desk's drawers.

He tried the handle and the safe popped open unexpectedly.

"Figures, no one locks up anything around here," he chortled, discovering nothing but old Wills and copies of Power of Attorneys.

The crafty burglar then moved to the library books. He rifled through them, pulling them out of their neat stacks and dumping them on the floor when he was done. There were no hidden compartments in any of them.

"Find it yet," Stew shouted up the stairs.

"No," Pete hollered back. "Go check the fridge and freezer."

"Okay, but we need to hurry. Melanie just texted me. She said an ambulance and a bunch of cop cars just got off the barge."

"Balls," Pete swore.

The oldest and fattest of the Mann brothers hoisted his beer belly and stuffed his shirt back in his pants as he contemplated where else Betty may have hidden the coin. Nothing stood out. There were no potted plants or odd decorations under which to hide something so small.

Who was this woman? Did she really have so little taste? The whole house was devoid of character; there were no knickknacks or memorabilia anywhere. He cursed Betty under his breath. The woman was an enigma.

Maybe the cop hid the coin in the barn with the pig, he realized with a start. The pig was nasty. The pig's stall would be a great place to hide something you didn't want found. He'd send his brother in. Stew didn't seem to mind the foul beast.

Pete returned to the bedroom and searched the dresser, the cupboards and under the pillows and mattress once more. He then went into the bathroom, pulled out a penknife, and sliced open a box of Maxi pads. He left the debris where it fell.

Satisfied that he had looked everywhere twice, he went downstairs.

Stew was pulling a frozen salmon and a package of hamburger out of the freezer along with a few bags of frozen French fries and peas. He looked behind and beneath them.

"Any luck?"

"No," Stew whined.

"Your friend sure lives a boring life," Pete bemoaned, not bothering to mention the pendant he had just stolen.

"That's because she's a nice lady," Stew retorted, his face reddening.

"Think she might have hidden it with the pig?"

"I doubt it," Stew snorted.

"Let's check the barn anyway," Pete snapped.

Stew put everything back in the freezer and followed his brother out the back door, not bothering to lock the door as it was open when they arrived.

The men strode quickly out to the barn. The light was already on.

"Betty's Jeep is gone," Stew said, nodding to the empty spot in the barn where tire tracks were visible in the dust on the floor.

"So what?"

"That means she left in a hurry. It also means once she's done with whatever's happening to warrant the police and an ambulance appearing at this time of night, that she'll be back, sooner rather than later," Stew scolded his brother.

"Then get in there," Pete pointed to Gertrude's stall, "and check it out."

Stew glared at his brother and then walked over to the pot-bellied pig's stall.

He looked over the door. Gertrude was asleep.

"Hey, Gertie," Stew said, reaching into the stall.

Gertrude squealed and hauled her great bulk to her feet. She sniffed his hand, hoping for a treat.

"Sorry, sweetie, no treats. Come by the pub tomorrow and I'll make you a grilled cheese."

"Good god, man, get in there and let's get going."

Stew unlocked the stall door and brushed past the pig. She snuffled his pockets, annoyed that no dog biscuits had been forthcoming. Stew pushed her snout away.

"What an ugly thing," his brother said, wiping his nose with a hanky. "It stinks."

"No more than what we're doing," Stew rumbled.

Stew searched beneath the hay and straw in Gertrude's stall, trying to avoid the steaming round piles of manure in the corner.

"There's nothing here either."

Stew's cell phone chimed. He looked at the second message from Melanie: "Fire at Tempest's house."

"What," his brother asked.

"There's a house fire down the street."

"Let's get out of here," Pete said.

"Finally," Stew moaned.

Stew gave Gertrude one last scratch before exiting her stall, forgetting to lock the door behind him as the Jersey cow mooed a greeting. The pub owner gave the cow a quick pat.

"We didn't check Peaches' stall," Stew said.

"You want to, go ahead, but if I wanted to keep a treasure safe, I'd stick with the pig," Pete snickered. He shook his head in disbelief as he stuck his hands in his pocket and fingered the small pendant. At least the evening wasn't a total bust.

"Naw, I'm done," Stew growled.

The brothers left, secure in the knowledge that they had searched every inch of Special Agent Betty Bruce's home. If they couldn't find the ancient coin, no one else could either.

***

Gertrude pushed the stall door open with her snout. She then peeked around the corner; the men had left. The pig wandered out into the aisle and then over to the open barn door. She saw Pete and Stew disappear around the side of the house, their footsteps receding as they continued down the lane.

She returned to her stall and snorted in dismay, her beady eyes glittering with mischief, the folds of flesh jiggling like Jello as she considered her options. She was wide awake now and more than a little miffed at Stew for waking her up without so much as a dog biscuit as a consolation prize.

Peaches lowered her head over the stall door so that the pig could nuzzle her.

Gertrude grunted and walked across the aisle.

The cow licked its lips.

The pig nosed the bolt that held the cow's door shut. It banged loosely against the loop that held it. Gertrude sank her teeth into the metal ring and pulled. The ring broke loose and the door popped open.

Gertrude whirled around, hooves click-clicking on the cement floor as she headed for the door. She stopped and squealed at her friend when the Jersey cow didn't immediately follow her.

It took a couple of attempts, but finally Gertrude managed to cajole the cow into joining her in an after dark excursion. It simply took a series of pitiful squeals and a headbutt or two.

***

Betty stopped in to see Reggie on the way home. When he didn't answer her soft knock on the door, she checked in with the manager in one of the greenhouses, a long-haired cherub faced twenty-something, who grinned and joked that she had worn the ole fella out. Betty simply smiled back at the young man and wished him a goodnight.

She drove the short distance home and then backed the Jeep into the barn.

"Oh, no," she said, seeing the open stall doors.

Betty struggled with the seat belt clasp, her tiredness making even the simplest task difficult. Finally, the seatbelt clasp clicked, freeing the lock, and the seatbelt rolled back into its holder. She pushed open the door and stepped out of the Jeep.

In the back seat, Champ's hair stood to attention. He let out a deep rumbling growl.

"I feel it to," she agreed, opening the rear door for the dog to exit the vehicle.

Champ jumped out, his nostrils quivering, his eyes alert. The dog put its nose to the ground. Champ traced the trail of the unknown intruders through the barn to Gertrude's stall.

The dog's reactions were puzzling. He whined, wagged his tail, and then growled, all in a short span of twenty feet.

The dog sat down, stared into Gertrude's empty stall for a moment, and then looked over his shoulder at Betty. He woofed, his tail wagging. He then whimpered and growled once again. If only the dog could talk.

Betty felt queasy. A shiver rippled up and down her spine. Gertrude couldn't possibly have opened the stall door on her own, and neither could Peaches.

Betty suspected that Champ was trying to tell her that someone they knew had been there. If so, why had they let Gertrude and Peaches out?

It couldn't have been her father. He would have left a note on the stall door.

It couldn't have been Reggie either as he was fast asleep.

Every nerve in her body tinkled. Adrenaline coursed through her veins. Her exhaustion dissipated.

"Come on, Champ, let's check the house," she told the dog. "In reality, Gertrude can look after herself and we know she'll protect Peaches if need be. They're probably down at the pub or at Dad's. Just because we didn't see her on the drive home, doesn't mean she's not there."

Betty pulled out her phone and dialed her father as she walked towards the house.

"Hey, Pops," she said when Archie answered on the second ring.

"Angel puss, what's going on? I've heard there's a fire at the Stewart's house and that the barge landed with a bunch of police cars on it."

Betty silently cursed the island grape vine.

"The chief has the fire under control and Tammy Smith passed away. Looks like a heart attack," she responded.

"Heck of a night," Archie replied, his voice breaking. "I liked Tammy. Pearl must be devastated."

"Pearl's okay. I told her myself. I didn't want her finding out the hard way," Betty answered her father. "Gertrude and Peaches aren't at your house, are they?"

"Not that I know of, but Vi and I will check just to make sure. You want me to bring them home if they are?"

"No, just shut the gate and keep them overnight. If I don't hear from you in the next few minutes, I'll assume they aren't there and are probably mooching off someone at the pub," Betty replied. "Gertie will come home when she's ready."

"Okay, then," her father said. "Get some sleep. It's been a long day for you."

"Thanks, Dad," she finished, ending the call.

Betty opened the back door. She glanced quickly around. Nothing seemed amiss.

Champ pushed past her. A snarl ripped through the shepherd and he took off barking, racing up the stairs two at a time.

Betty ran after the dog, once again wishing that she had her service pistol. She had decided to turn it in on her last day of work, not thinking she'd ever need it on Seal Island.

Champ barreled through the hallway and turned left into the study, Betty right on his heels.

Betty gasped. The study was a mess. There were books scattered across the floor. The desk drawers were wide open, the papers she had been working on left askew.

She snorted in disgust. She fingered the gold coin in her pocket. She knew the break-in was related. Someone had been looking for it.

"Good boy," she muttered, stroking the dog's back. "I give you permission to bite the so-and-so when we find him. After that, we'll get Reggie to make him walk the plank."

The dog whined and wagged its tail.

Betty checked the spare bedrooms, her own bedroom last. The spare bedrooms were fine, but her room was trashed and so was her private bathroom. She checked her jewellery: the small pearl and diamond heart pendant was gone. She didn't care about it anyway. Her ex-husband had given it to her a few days after she told him she wanted a divorce. Still, it was the principle of the whole thing.

"Buggers," she growled.

The dog at her side growled too, sensing its master's anger.

Betty thought of calling Singh, especially while he was here, but she preferred to deal with Tom Powder on this. That, and she really was dead on her feet, the adrenaline needle fixed on empty. The thought of a forensic crew and dozen police officers traipsing through her house right now made her feel ill. She doubted they'd find anything, and the damage to her personal space had already been done.

Betty ripped the sheets and pillows off the bed. There was no way she was going to sleep on a bed rifled by a thief, or thieves.

Betty's blue eyes were a blaze. Her normally serene face was red. Sweat dripped from her brow. She needed this like a hole in the head. She thanked the good Lord that she had kept the coin with her and that her father and Vi were fine.

The dog padded after her as she went back down the stairs, her arms full of sheets and pillowcases. The laundry room was on the main floor of the house.

The question was should she go off in search of her pig and cow or just collapse? Yes, Gertrude could look after herself, but that was before Betty had discovered that her house had been tossed. Her father hadn't called so they weren't there. She could try the pub, but did she really feel like going down to retrieve them? There would be questions galore about the fire and police arrival.

Betty stuffed the linen into the washer and turned it on. She sighed wearily; her decision made. She couldn't live with herself if she didn't make at least one more call.

She dialed the pub. It was prime tourist season after all and who knew what havoc Gertrude and Peaches were creating if they were there. She was surprised when Melanie answered.

"Hey, Mel, is Stew there," Betty asked the part-time bartender/part-time farm helper.

"No, I don't know where he is," Melanie replied. "He called me in asking me to fill in for awhile. Everyone's a buzz about the fire and the police cars arrival."

Betty could hear the din of happy patrons in the background.

"Sorry, I know you're busy, but is Gertie and Peaches down there," Betty asked.

"Hang on," Melanie said. "Oh, wait, there's Stew and his brother now. I'll ask them."

Betty heard Melanie shout to Stew, asking if Gertrude was outside. She didn't hear Stew's response.

"Stew says that they're not," Melanie yelled, the crowd behind her getting louder as they called out to Stew asking what was going on.

"Okay, thanks," Betty said tiredly.

"Hey, what's going on? Do you know," Melanie said, her voice so loud that Betty had to hold the phone away from her ear.

"There's a fire at the Stewart house, but its under control, and Tammy Smith just passed away from what appears to be natural causes," Betty answered, not wanting to say too much about Tammy's death.

"Oh, that's so sad. I'll let Stew know," Melanie said. "I've got to go. This place is crazy."

"No probs, thanks again, Mel," Betty finished.

Complete exhaustion overtook her. Betty reeled sideways. She grabbed a counter for support. The room was spinning, faster and faster.

Betty staggered to the kitchen and poured herself a glass of water.

The dog whimpered.

"Sorry, buddy."

Betty filled his water bowl and gave him some kibble. She then locked the back and front door and stumbled to the living room couch. She'd deal with the study, her bedroom, the whereabouts of her pig and cow, and her call to Tom Powder in the morning.

She laid down on the couch, tucked a pillow under her head, and was fast asleep in no time.

The German shepherd crawled onto the end of the couch, pushed between her legs, and rested its head on Betty's stomach. Champ stared lovingly at his master, total devotion in his eyes.

Pig Hunt

"Was that your special agent," Pete whispered in his brother's ear.

"Yes," Stew replied. "Why?"

Pete glanced around, making sure no one was listening.

Bar stools were filled with locals sharing a pint and gossiping about the current goings on, Morris Tweedsmuir and his sister, Alana, among them. Alana was as gaunt and red-headed as her brother. The regular tables were filled with sunburned tourists. Executives and their wives laughed and gobbled down copious amounts of beer with their fish and chips, having exchanged business suits for white shorts, colorful shirts, and leather sandals.

No one seemed the slightest bit interested in the two men as they brushed by Melanie who stood behind the bar drawing out glass after glass of draft as fast as she could.

"She just asked about the pig, didn't she?" Pete hissed.

"So?"

"So maybe we should follow it? Maybe it'll take us to the treasure," the fat man said breathlessly, his heart racing at the thought of all the gold coins ripe for the picking if they played their cards right.

"That's a bloody good idea," Stew exclaimed.

"Shhhh," his brother shushed him.

"Mel, I know it's busy, but can you continue to hold down the fort me," Stew asked the pretty bartender.

"If the price is right, I can," she joked.

"Done," the barrel-chested pub owner said. "Anything you want, you got it."

"You don't even know what I want yet," Melanie purred.

"Whatever it is, you can have it," Stew grinned. "You're priceless."

Morris, Alana, and a handful of locals cheered.

"The last time you said that," Melanie cooed, fixing him with a steady gaze, "your wife tried to shoot me."

"But she missed and now she's safely behind bars," Stew chortled.

"And one day she's going to be back, but I intend to be married off by then," Melanie bantered back.

"Promises, promises," the pub owner laughed. "How is that new beau of yours working out? Keeping you on the straight and narrow? If not, my door is always open."

Melanie and the bar patrons roared with laughter.

"That's enough, little brother," Pete mumbled, tugging his brother out from behind the bar.

"I'm coming. Just having a bit of fun."

"That's the problem," his brother hissed. "That's what got you into your financial mess in the first place."

"Not any more," Stew grinned, eyeing the happy crowd.

Stew smiled at everyone he passed as he and Pete headed for the door. Each person near him tugged at his sleeve asking for information on the goings-on, until Pete shot them a menacing look, then they'd switch their conversation to Stew's crazy brother.

***

"Did you see that," Alana whispered to her brother.

"See what," Morris replied.

"They're up to something."

"How do you know," Morris queried.

"Melanie just asked if Stew had seen Gertrude, and then all of a sudden Stew has to go someplace urgent," she said, leaning in close to her brother. "Seems to me like they might know where Gertrude is at."

"Find the pig; find the treasure," Morris gasped, his grey eyes twinkling.

"Exactly."

"What's our tab," Morris asked the bartender.

"You two aren't going to wait to see if the coppers or the fire brigade come in and fill us in," Melanie countered, surprized.

"We've got a couple of goats that're probably going to birth tonight," Alana lied.

"Oh, make sure you let me know when they've arrived," Melanie purred, handing Morris his bill. "I'd love to come see them."

"We'll do that," Morris replied, paying his tab with a couple of torn twenty-dollar bills. "Rest is for you."

"Thanks guys. Have a good evening."

Morris and his sister grinned crookedly as they left the pub.

"What's the plan," Morris asked Alana, looking left and then right for signs of Gertrude or Peaches, the latter never being far behind the first.

The marina was as brightly lit as the Milky Way on a clear Winter's night. Lights were on in almost all the cabins of the pleasure craft moored at the dock and in the bay. The windows in Reggie's boat, *Persephone*, were dark as were the other fishing trawlers tied up close to him. Morris knew that Gertrude would have no interest in being out on the docks, not without Reggie.

The white sided artisan tents along the boardwalk were zipped up tight, tent flaps down. The General Store was closed too, a red security light visible inside the large window.

"I say we follow along after those blokes unless we see Gertie first," Alana nodded towards the two men striding purposefully up North Shore Road, the beam from a flashlight illuminating their way.

"They do seem to know where they're headed, don't they," Morris grinned at his sister.

The pair raced after the two brothers, carefully keeping to the side of the road, where the shadows hid them from view and the dirt muffled their footfalls.

As they approached the trail that split off from the main road to the beach, Morris thought he heard a cow moo.

"Did you hear that," Morris gasped, skidding to a stop.

"I didn't hear anything," Alana replied.

"There! Hear it?

The two listened intently.

A faint moo echoed through the night.

"Where's it coming from?"

"The beach, I think," Morris said, motioning his sister down the trail. "Wherever Peaches is, Gertrude is."

"You sure that was Peaches?" Alana asked impatiently.

"What other cow do you know would be down at the beach this late at night?"

"Point taken."

Morris pulled a set of keys from his pocket. He turned on a small penlight and aimed it at the root strewn trail.

"Come on, let's go," he told his sister.

"Maybe one of us should follow those two," she said, nodding towards Stew and Pete Mann whose shadows were quickly fading into the dark.

"Okay. You take the penlight and check the beach. If Gertie and Peaches are there, follow them. They may indeed head back to where Gertie found that coin. I'll follow the brothers Mann. I'd rather me follow them than you. I don't like that Pete fella very much."

"I'm down with that, bro," his sister agreed.

Morris handed Alana his keys and then jogged off after the Mann brothers.

She whisked the penlight back and forth over the narrow forest trail as she headed towards the beach in search of the wayward pot-bellied pig and the Jersey cow.

Alana stopped when she reached the beach. The wind ruffled her hair and the crowns of the trees overhead. Waves splashed against the rocky shore.

She frowned.

There!

In the distance, she heard Peaches moo, a beseeching cry, both sharp and frightened at the same time.

Alana increased her pace.

***

Two inebriated young men stood on the patio outside the pub, leaning against the railing, in the shadows of the eavestrough at the end of the deck.

"And where do you think those folks are going," one of the young men asked the other.

"Me thinks we've got us a pig hunt, Sherlock," the shorter of the two replied.

"I believe you're right, Doctor Watson," he agreed.

"Shall we join in the fun, Detective?"

"We shall."

The young men elbowed each other, putting their night of debauchery on hold, the lure of gold taking over their better judgement.

They laughed as they stumbled off the porch.

The lowest estimate of the value of the treasure that someone gave them in the pub was three million dollars, and the highest estimate was seven million.

That was a lot of mullah for two students awash in university debt.

***

"Where do you think that thing might have gone," Pete rumbled.

"By that 'thing', I'm guessing you mean Gertrude," Stew chortled.

"Whatever. You know it. Think like it," Pete commanded his brother.

If it hadn't been so dark Stew would have seen the vile look his brother cast upon him and probably would have turned around. Because he didn't, he responded with some brevity.

"Gertrude's favorite spots are my pub, Reggie's boat, the beach by the pier, Vi Bone's house, Archie's place of course, Rainbow and Frank McDonald's farm, and I believe Pearl Tullis and Tammy Smith's homesteads. The ladies are known for sharing high tea with her."

"How do you know all that," Pete asked, his temper easing.

"Because folks around here like me, big brother," Stew chortled, "and they love to talk about that pig. You should try opening up a bit. Folks are already giving you a wide berth. Haven't you noticed."

Pete guffawed. Islanders were mad as hatters in his opinion. They should all be keeping their distance from him, except for that peachy bartender. She was spunky. He liked that in a woman, not the dull wishy-washy kind of female that Betty Bruce appeared to be. Once he had that treasure, he was sure Melanie would stop sidling away from him.

"Where should we look first," Pete asked.

"We missed the beach turn-off. The tide is coming in, so I doubt Gertie would be beachcombing anyway. She prefers the low tide. There's more to rummage through. Vi's place is just up ahead," Stew replied, scratching his day-old whiskers. "She could be there."

"We'll start there then. The judge is a friend of yours, isn't she? It'll give us an excuse to visit if she sees us."

"I like to think so," Stew mumbled, not altogether sure. The two had their differences in the last year.

***

Stew flicked his flashlight over the 'Bone's Bailiwick' sign that hung in front of the driveway. The sign gave the clifftop cottage some character in Stew's estimation.

Vi's brother, Wally, had carved the sign out of a large maple burl years ago. Stew thought it was a handsome thing, hardly weathered at all. Vi had taken it down when she had briefly listed the house for sale but put it back up when she decided to stay.

"This way," Stew directed his brother.

The a-frame style log cottage known locally as Bone's Bailiwick stood on a cliff top facing Vancouver Island. The view was spectacular on a clear day.

Two porch lights illuminated the cobbled path leading to the rear garden and back porch. The glow from the light cast soft shadows on the tall sunflowers and decimated flowers that lined the entry way. Stew noted that Peaches had done a good job at eating her way through the tulips and geraniums.

The vegetable garden was fenced all the way around with six-foot-high deer fencing which also deterred pot-bellied pigs, Jersey cows, and the wild sheep and goats that roamed the forests.

"I don't see her," Stew commented dryly.

Pete grunted and turned around. Stew followed suit.

There was a flash of movement beside the driveway, closer to the road. The dark shadows beneath the trees moved faster than the night's breeze would allow for. The moving shadows were too tall and narrow to be the pig or the cow.

"You see that," Pete whispered to his brother.

"I did," Stew agreed. "Think we're being followed?"

Pete grimaced, his face darkening.

Stew gulped. His brother had a temper. Sometimes, Stew was afraid of him.

"Want to confront him," Stew stammered.

"Let it play out," his brother snickered.

***

Alana crept silently along the trail until she reached the beach head. This was the spot where the woman's body everyone called *The Painted Lady* had washed up on shore. It was also the place where Gertrude had discovered a severed foot in a sneaker, just one of many that had washed up on the shores of several islands in the Strait of Georgia. The thought made Alana shiver.

She flashed the beam from the penlight over the rocky beach. The tide was quickly coming in; the water rising. It was hard to walk along the beach because of the logs and the piles of seaweed packed tightly against them.

The narrow beam from her penlight reflected against the cream-colored coat of a large animal. She started towards it, using the long giant logs, some four to five feet in diameter, as balance beams to keep from getting wet.

A slow smile creased her lips as she approached the two animals.

She flashed the penlight over the cow's face. The Jersey cow looked miserable, her tail dragging in the surf, her legs and hooves buried in the churning water.

The pot-bellied pig strolled casually atop the downed logs, walking carelessly along as if the world was her oyster, completely oblivious to the fact that her friend's hooves weren't built for log scaling.

Alana giggled. She wished her brother was here. He would have loved it.

If she turned the penlight on herself, what would she look like? Would her eyes look as deep and baleful as the cow's or would they look as alive and intelligent as the pig's?

Alana laughed aloud.

She was being silly, she knew, but couldn't help herself.

She imagined herself as a wild Scottish maid, standing on beach beneath a star filled night just like this, searching the waves for signs of the ship that bore her handsome captain home, the wind lifting her hair into a delightful wave of red curls the envy of every mermaid in the vicinity.

She flung one hand dramatically over her brow while the other brushed out an imaginary skirt. She tossed her head, her hair billowing out behind her. She then stood still, poised upon the log, the picture of an innocent wife longing for her captain.

Alana broke her stance.

She started laughing. She laughed so hard she couldn't breathe. She had to stop reading Andy MacDowell's torchy historical romance novels.

The young woman wiped away her tears with the hem of her shirt and then followed discreetly after her quarry, keeping a respectable distance between the lumberjack pig and the waterlogged cow. She knew that they would have to either circle back the way they had come or find another way up the cliff as Peaches would be swimming soon.

***

Morris knelt behind a juniper bush on the south side of the road facing the driveway into Vi Bone's cottage. He knew the pig and cow weren't there. They were on the beach. His sister had that covered.

Morris also knew that Stew and his brother were up to something. Stew's brother seemed to know an awful lot about the coin's value. He didn't know what the man did for a living, but Morris recognized a con man when he saw one and Pete Mann was that, or worse.

What am I doing here, he wondered? It was Gertie who'd lead him to the gold, not the brothers Mann.

The sound of muffled laughter drifted towards him. Two young men staggered drunkenly up the road. They weren't very stealthy. They used their cell phones to light their way. One of them skewed sideways as if he was on the deck of the Titanic right before it went down. The other boy pushed him back upright just in time.

"I think they went that-a-way," the taller boy said, pointing towards Bone's Bailiwick.

"After you," the other one said, bowing to his friend.

"No after you," the first boy bowed back, faking an English accent.

The boys giggled as they repeated the action, clunking heads together in the process. With one final bow, the two lurched into the trees beside the driveway. Leaves and broken branches snapped under foot. The light from their cell phones flickered through the foliage. The boys then started to use their phones as light sabres.

Morris groaned. The drunken sods thought they were Jedi knights, out on some quest. That was just what he needed. The two idiots were screwing everything up.

There was no way that Stew and his brother couldn't hear or see them.

Morris slowed his breathing and eased himself deeper into the bush, not wanting to be seen.

The boys finally clued in that they were supposed to be hiding and turned off their cell phones, but the damage was already done.

"Hey, you, come out of there," Pete Mann bellowed, shining his flashlight into the trees.

"Come on out," Stew echoed.

The Mann brothers' flashlights illuminated the startled faces of the two young men.

Like two bear cups frolicking in the forest, the pair cavorted out onto the driveway, sporting silly grins, their nose and eyes red from too much alcohol.

"We just wanted to find the treasure," the tallest young man declared, his body weaving in space like a bowling pin that had just been clipped by a bowling ball. It was a toss up as to which way he would fall.

"Yeah, and we think you guys know where it is," the short one sneered.

"You think so, do you," the fat man glowered.

"We do," the tall one replied.

"Ah, they're just drunk, bro," Stew chortled.

"That we are," the little guy agreed.

The two boys started laughing. Stew joined in.

To Morris and everyone else's surprise, Pete pulled a small revolver out from behind his back and pointed it at the two young men.

"What the heck are you doing," Stew gasped. "Put that away."

Morris felt his heart sink. He was right about Pete Mann. He was bad news. Morris was glad he had sent his sister off to the beach without him.

"I want you two boys to get back on the boat you came here on and vamoose," Pete threatened. "You will forget about us, forget about the treasure, and not come back to Seal Island again. Do you hear me?"

"You won't shoot us," the taller boy slurred.

"Yeah, we're unarmed. That'd be murder," the little one agreed.

"That's if they find your bodies," Pete drawled, his eyes glittering in the back light cast by the flashlight.

Something about his tone finally got through to the frat boys. Their faces sobered. Their eyes focused on the round black muzzle of the gun pointing at them.

Morris saw Stew begin to sweat.

The rumble of a big truck rattled Morris' already fried nerves. He dove to the ground as the island's fire truck thundered down the road.

Pete quickly whisked his revolver out of sight.

Stew wiped the sweat from his face with the back of one hand.

The boys crashed out of the bush and into the path of the fire truck. Brakes squealed. The fire truck came to a screeching halt.

"STOP," the tall boy screamed.

"He's going to kill us," the other one shouted.

The fire chief jumped out of the truck.

"You almost got killed alright, but by Big Red," the fire chief yelled angrily, nodding towards the giant fire truck. "What the blue blazes are you doing jumping out of the bushes in front of our truck at this hour?"

Morris couldn't agree with the chief more.

"That guy over there has a gun!"

The fire chief turned towards where the university student was pointing, but there was no one there.

Stew and Pete Mann were gone. Morris figured they either ran into the forest or hid behind Vi's house.

"There's no one there."

The boys looked confused.

"But he was there," the tall boy whined.

"Really, he was," the short one pouted.

"I think you gents have had a few too many pints at the Bristling Boar. It's all that talk of treasure everyone is going on about," the fire chief muttered. "Get in the back of the truck. I'm taking you back to the marina. You can figure out where to go from there."

"But we're on a pig hunt," they said in unison.

"A pig hunt, eh," the fire chief chuckled. "That pig you're hunting has more brains than you. Now, climb aboard or I'll call the cops. I hear they're still on the island."

"But...," the tall boy whimpered.

"Drunk tank or marina? Your choice," the fire chief barked at them.

Morris didn't know they had a drunk tank on the island.

The two young men skulked over to the fire truck. Two firefighters offered them a hand.

"Can we at least go back with the sirens on," the short young man grinned.

The chief and fire crew laughed as they buckled in the intoxicated pair of students.

The fire truck's driver grinned as he flipped on the lights and drove away. A swirling candy cane of red and white lights bounced off the trees.

Morris sank deeper into the pile of dead leaves he was laying on. He prayed that no one would see him. He tucked his head down into the earth and held his breath. A cricket crawled up his chin, across his cheek, and settled on his nose. He desperately fought the urge to sneeze.

Pete and Stew clambered out from behind a couple of tall cedars as the fire truck's taillights retreated into the distance.

"You never said anything about a gun," Stew fumed.

"You think we won't need one? There are going to be way worse types than those drunken sods descending upon this island," Pete retorted. "Gold fever's going to hit and it's going to hit hard. We'll run out of time if we don't find that damn pig and cow in a hurry."

"I don't care," Stew simmered. "You want to go charging off in search of a treasure that probably doesn't exist, go ahead. Count me out."

Stew turned on his flashlight and barrelled down the road, leaving his brother to fend for himself.

The fat man swore and stalked off after him.

Morris let out his breath and brushed the cricket from his nose, scratching the spot raw where it had been.

He waited until he couldn't see either of the men before standing up and brushing himself off. He walked quickly in the opposite direction of the men, making sure he kept to the shadows at the side of the road. The moon was now peeking out from behind Watchtower Mountain, so the road was a ribbon of moonlight.

If he didn't meet up with Alana before he got to the entrance to the McDonald farm, he would backtrack until he found the deer trail that wound around the base of Watchtower Mountain and ended at South Shore Road. It was going to be a long walk home, but it was a nice night and the stars were bright.

***

Alana never thought she'd be grateful for being able to walk in a pig's footsteps, but she was. She followed the pig's hoofprints, carefully selecting where Gertrude had placed one foot after the other on the slippery logs.

The cow mooed piteously in the quickly rising surf.

Alana agreed with the cow's sentiment. She was tired and her back ached from the awkward angles she was having to walk at. The wind and waves had chased the heroine out of her about four logs ago.

The pig slipped off the log. It landed in the surf with a crash. Gertrude nosed Peaches as if looking for support, but the cow wanted none of her. Alana knew the feeling. She wasn't impressed either.

The thrill of the adventure had faded. Alana wanted to go home.

She had no idea where Gertrude was leading them until the pig climbed onto a wide cement boat ramp. Peaches let out a loud grunt as she hauled her great bulk out of the surf onto the platform and surged forward after Gertrude, her long legs almost buckling beneath her.

Alana sympathized with Peaches. Her calf muscles were screaming.

Winded, Alana stood silently for a moment catching her breath. She looked up. A wide path zig-zagged from the top of the hill down to the water. It was only about one hundred feet to the top. To her left, a jetty of land poked a crooked finger out to sea in a come-hither gesture. She thought she saw the dark outline of a gazebo on the jetty's edge.

The lithe young woman climbed onto the cement ramp and then followed the animals up the path to the top of the incline.

A vast expanse of cultured gardens stretched outwards. Pink, red, and white azalea and rhododendron bushes bloomed everywhere. A grey slate stone path meandered between the flowering bushes. Several Japanese maples shaded bouquets of purple heather and pink hyacinths.

Alana thought the air smelled like baclava; it was so full of honey-like nectar from all the flowers.

She followed the sound of the animal's hooves clicking against the paver stones, through the garden, around a bend, and to a great fountain guarded by the biggest stone angel Alana had ever seen.

Alana paled.

She knew that stone angel and she knew whose garden that it watched over.

Alana walked around the fountain, the beam from her tiny penlight traveling upwards across the angel's skirts to its upraised arms and serene face. This was the angel in whose arms Summer River gasped her last breath.

Gertrude grunted.

Alana lowered her penlight.

The pig stood there, glaring at her. Its eyes were hooded. If a pig could frown, then Gertrude was doing so.

"I'm sorry," Alana stammered. She had no idea why she felt she needed to apologize to the pot-bellied pig, but she did anyway.

Gertrude huffed and snorted. She then spun around and trotted off into the dark.

Alana searched the beseeching face of the stone angel. The soulless look in the alabaster eyes made her skin crawl. A cold breeze brushed against her face. She shivered uncontrollably.

Was that the ghost of Summer River brushing against her?

Alana raced after Gertrude, running across the garden, and around the side of the vacant house. She skidded to a stop, arms wind milling as she almost cartwheeled over top of the pot-bellied pig who had stopped and was now snuffling around the base a massive oak tree.

There was a three-foot by two-foot hole dug beneath the roots of the tree. Gertrude snuffled around the hole and then the base of the tree, looking for truffles. The pig grunted and groaned as it foraged for food.

The pig made a lot of noise. Alana wasn't worried though. Barney Whyte owned the property she was skulking about on, along with a voracious pot-bellied pig and cow. He and his wife were in jail.

"Is this it," Alana cried breathlessly. "Is this where you found it, girl?"

Alana knelt beside the pig and started digging in the earth.

"Ooooohhh, yuck," she stuttered, her hands coming away sticky with moldy truffles.

Gertrude gobbled them off her fingers.

Alana steeled herself and continued to dig but found nothing but black truffles and earthy loam.

She sat back on her haunches, defeated.

"This isn't the place is it," she asked the pig. "The only treasure here is yours."

Gertrude snorted and nuzzled her face. The pig left a black streak of rotten truffle fuzz across Alana's cheek.

Alana started to laugh.

"So now I'm your best friend, eh," she giggled. "Well, I think I've had enough treasure hunting for the night. Unless you want to wait until morning when the tide goes out, I suggest you and Peaches come with me. I'll open up the gate."

The pig's tail wind milled as it watched its newfound best friend walk away. The cow completely ignored them both.

Alana unfastened the clasp on the front gate and held it open.

"Are you coming," she called.

The pig wrinkled its snout, whiskers quivering and then squealed, racing towards the young red-haired woman.

The cow chewed on a rose bud.

"Come on Peaches, let's go home."

The cow walked slowly towards her, its tail flicking from side to side, big black eyes shining like onyx within a ghostly face as the shadows in the garden elongated behind it.

Alana laughed merrily as she closed and locked the gate behind her. She may not have found the sorcerer's gold, but she had shared an adventure with Gertrude and Peaches that would be the envy of many an island resident.

In the garden, the face of the stone angel was turned towards the sea, the moonlight creating a heavenly aura about it. A cloud brushed against the moon. The angel's sightless eyes appeared to blink.

Alana flicked off the penlight and moseyed back down North Shore Road, heading towards Betty's house, the moon lighting her way. She didn't know that she had missed her brother by about thirty minutes.

"I'll drop you guys at home and then I think I'll stay at Mel's," Alana said to Gertrude. "She's sleeping on Reggie's boat tonight. He won't mind if I sleep there too. Believe me, Gert, couch surfing is no fun even if it is on a pretty swanky trawler in the harbor."

The pig snuffled her fingers, trying to lick the last bit of truffle dust off them.

Alana chuckled and stuffed her hands in her pockets, not wanting to lose any apendages to a spoiled pig.

Gold Fever

The Blue Heeler whined and danced by the front door, anxious to be let out.

Rainbow yawned and opened the door for the dog. The dog raced off towards the beach, barking furiously.

She glanced outside at the sun dappled garden and dew-covered garden. The air was fresh and brisk. Rainbow decided to leave the door open.

"What's Blue up to," Frank asked, walking into the kitchen in nothing but his underwear. He too yawned and stretched.

"Jeepers, it's only six thirty," Frank grumbled. "Even for us, that's early."

"Probably after a rabbit," Rainbow said sleepily. "I'll put some water on to boil. You want tea or coffee this morning?"

"Coffee for me, babe," Frank replied as he walked over to kiss his wife on the cheek before shuffling back to the bedroom to get dressed.

Rainbow grinned and then filled the kettle, her long dreadlocks falling about her face and shoulders. She absently pulled a hair tie from her robe pocket and tied her hair up.

"I can still hear Blue barking," Frank yelled from the bedroom.

"Guess I better get dressed as well," she mumbled.

"What's that," Frank queried, walking back into the kitchen dressed in frayed denim shorts and a Blue Jay's t-shirt.

"I said, I guess I better get dressed too so we can go see what all the fuss is about," she grinned.

Rainbow wrapped her arms around her husband's waist and stared up into his brown eyes and unruly mop of hair. His hair was now sun-bleached with stripes of red and blond shimmering amid the brown curly locks. He had let his hair grow out to shoulder length and she found it sexy.

"You keep staring at me like that and the dog and birds will have to wait," he whispered huskily.

Rainbow laughed and kissed him passionately, before breaking away and sashaying off to the bedroom.

The kettle on the gas stove began to whistle.

Frank smiled as he poured himself a cup of coffee. He added a dollop of honey to the thick black cup of brew.

Outside, the sun was shining, its rays creating a kaleidoscope pattern of white and gold on the hardwood floors in the kitchen.

Rainbow wandered back into the kitchen wearing khaki coloured hemp culottes, sandals, and a bright yellow, pink and purple tie-dyed blouse.

The look in Frank's eyes made Rainbow smile.

"It's a beautiful day," Frank teased.

"Yes, it is," she purred.

Frank leaned against the kitchen counter, staring out the door at the fields he had just ploughed the day before while his wife made a pot of Oolong tea.

"There's a light mist hovering over the meadow I turned over with the tractor yesterday. The earth looks like wet coffee grounds. I can't wait to get at it," Frank said excitedly.

"You're very poetic this morning," Rainbow chuckled, looking past her husband to the beautiful morning outside. "You're right though, it does look like wet coffee grounds."

Rainbow poured herself a cup of tea.

"I can't wait until the Oolong, Green tea, and Black tea are big enough to harvest. I want to expand the Lavender and Chamomile lines too. You know I already have a waiting list of customers and some of the hotels and spas that Summer used to sell to had called me," Rainbow added, snaking an around his waist.

Frank planted a brief kiss on top of her head.

Rainbow sighed with pleasure.

"I'm so happy we bought this farm," she whispered.

"Me too," he agreed.

Rainbow missed her pet psychic and dog training business. The herb and tea business took up too much of her time to do both. She made incredible money in her booth at the weekend markets. The islanders had embraced the couple since they had continued to sell some of Summer River's lines of specialty teas now re-branded under the McDonald Farm's banner.

Rainbow beamed; her heart swelled with love.

"Penny for your thoughts," Frank murmured in her ear.

"I was just thinking how lucky we are. I am so thankful that Summer's ghost seems to be at rest and there is so much positive energy in this house and on the farm now."

"Despite the rocky start," Frank blushed.

"Despite the rocky start," she grinned and then pushed him delicately towards to door. "Don't you have some fowl to feed?"

"I do, but I was rather comfortable wrapped up in the arms of my oh so beautiful wife."

Rainbow laughed.

The dog's barking grew louder and more furious.

"I better see what's got Blue going first," Frank said.

"I hope racoons haven't gotten into the bird pens," she fretted.

"You're right," he gasped, suddenly wide awake. "I better move it."

Frank put his cup of coffee on the counter and raced out the door.

Rainbow knew she should go with her husband to see if there were any wounded birds that needed tending, but if a racoon had gotten into the pens, she didn't want to see the slaughter. Frank would call her if he needed her.

***

Frank charged towards the barn, checking the chicken and Cornish hen pens first. The brown and white birds clucked furiously when they spotted him, demanding their morning grain. There were no dead hens or roosters or any signs of broken wire.

Frank then checked the duck pen. Most of the Muscovy and Peking ducks floated in the small pond he had dug for them. They were a colorful lot. They quacked a greeting, unconcerned. Others rested on the bank and a few nested in the nesting huts.

Frank let out a sigh of relief.

The dog continued to bark furiously.

"What has gotten into you this morning, Blue," he grumbled as he jogged down the short hill to the beach.

What he saw there made him stop short.

No wonder the dog was in a frenzy!

The beach looked like Normandy Beach after the Allied invasion in World War II. There were holes everywhere.

There had to be at least a hundred people scurrying around the small crescent of beach and shoreline that edged the farm's boundary, more than half of them with metal detectors. They swept back and forth with the instruments, shouting with glee when one of the metal detector's beeped. People descended like a pack of hyenas upon the person whose detector went off.

The cove was filled with boats, kayaks, and dinghies. Some were moored, others were pulled up on the sand or on rocky shoals left bare by the out-going tide.

Blue barked up a storm, racing between the treasure hunters, unsure about what to do.

Frank whistled for the heeler.

Blue galloped back to him. The dog circled him frantically, unable to sit or lay down, panting laboriously, a steady stream of drool dripping from its mouth.

Two men carrying shovels and a woman carrying a metal detector started marching up the slope leading onto the lower half of his property.

"Hey, this is private property," he shouted, running towards them.

The woman flipped him the bird.

The dog barked angrily at her.

"Get the Hell off my land," Frank swore, his anger rising as the three continued to ignore him.

"Good luck, buddy," the man wearing a grey fedora and loud Bermuda shirt glowered.

"That's it, I'm calling the cops," Frank fumed. "You're all trespassing."

"No, we're not," the woman who had flipped him the bird croaked. "We're still on the tideline. You don't own that."

Frank's face turned as red as the woman's sunburn.

"You set one foot past the tideline and I'll sick the dog on you," Frank spat, reassuring the dog with a friendly pat. He would never put his dog in that kind of jeopardy, but these bozos didn't know that. He also knew the dog would never bite anyone; it wasn't in Blue's nature. Still, he was angry, and it was the only thing he could think of to say.

"Then we'll call the cops on you," Bermuda shirt declared, slamming the shovel into the ground.

Out on the beach, a fight had broken out.

It was time to call Betty.

Frank shook his head and spun around, racing up the hill.

"Blue, come!"

The dog whined and then galloped up the trail after Frank.

***

Pearl rose with the sunrise, as much by habit as the sleepless night that the death of her friend had caused.

The old woman made herself a large pot of tea and then wrapped a woolen shawl around her shoulders. She placed the teapot on a tray beside two chipped china teacups with tiny pink roses on them, and a hand pottered milk jug and honey pot. She then carried the tray outside, placing it on a rustic log table, before sitting down in her old rocker. Her father had made the rocker out of willow branches thirty years-ago and it was still as strong as the day it was fashioned.

A million tiny prisms of light reflected prettily in the dewdrops on the spiderwebs and leaves of the flowers and foliage within her garden.

Pearl tipped her face towards the sun, inhaling the wonderful scents that filled the air, and revelling in the warm glow. It would be too hot to do so by mid-afternoon.

Pearl sighed, her shoulders drooping. She could sense her friend's presence beside her. It was comforting, but not the same as having Tammy sitting across the log table from her reminiscing about when they were young or sharing gossip about who was sleeping with whom on the island.

She poured tea into the two china cups, and then sat back in her rocker listening to the morning birds sing. The wind was non-existent. It was a beautiful morning.

A deep sorrow mixed with a tinge of guilt caused a tear to slip from one eye.

Pearl brushed it away.

She missed her friend with all her heart and soul.

For the past twenty-five years Tammy had joined her for an early morning tea in the garden. Neither rain, sun, sleet nor snow, kept the two from enjoying one of life's simpler pleasures. Summer River used to join them during the off-season, but then she too had died. Pearl missed the hippy flowerchild as much as Tammy. She had been a charming girl.

Pearl grimaced. It seemed that her lot in life was to outlive all her friends. Oh, well, so be it, she thought.

Just the other day, Rainbow McDonald told her that Summer's ghost had visited her several times, but that Summer was at rest now having finally gone over to join her fiancé and parents on the other side.

Pearl wasn't as certain about that as Rainbow had been.

What if Summer was here now? What if Summer was standing beside Tammy? Just because Pearl couldn't see them, didn't mean the two spirits weren't enjoying the garden this morning with her. How rude of her not to have brought out a third teacup. She vowed that tomorrow she would. It would be her new morning ritual. Tea with the angels.

Pearl laughed lightly.

She was getting dotty in her old age.

It seemed fitting that Rainbow McDonald paid Pearl regular visits given that the McDonald's had bought Summer's farm after Summer died so tragically. Pearl knew that Summer would be pleased. That was probably why Rainbow had seen her ghost.

A trio of voices floated towards her like the whisper of lovers in the night. She couldn't quite make out what the three people were saying until they walked by her garden fence.

"Why don't we ask the old lady," Pearl heard a teenaged boy ask his companion as they got closer.

"Like she's going to tell us where its buried if she knows," another boy retorted.

"Can't hurt," quipped a young girl.

Pearl grinned. She wished she could see the three young scallywags.

Soon, she told herself, *soon.*

"It's gold you're looking for, is it," she cackled. Even to her ears, she sounded like a witch out of Shakespeare's *Macbeth.* That lifted her spirits in heartbeat. She had always dreamed of being an actress. Maybe she'd have a little fun with the kids.

"You know where it is," one of the boys asked. His voice was still high, not having broken yet. Pearl guessed him to be about twelve.

"Manners, children," Pearl called. "Come in through the gate so I don't have to yell."

The three teens entered the rose garden, leaving the gate open behind them.

"Why do you have two cups of tea out," the second boy asked, leaning forward to investigate the house through the open door. "Is there someone else here?"

"No, there's nobody but me, a crazy old lady. I lost my best friend last night," Pearl confessed.

"That's harsh," said the young girl.

"It is," Pearl agreed. "We had tea together every morning for more years than you or your mother have been on this earth. The tea is my way of honoring her."

"That's really sweet," the young girl replied.

"I was thinking of adding another teacup for another friend who is no longer here. What do you think of that," she asked the girl, sensing a kindred spirit.

"Why not," the girl said in a pretty voice that would soon have the boys swooning over her; that is, if they already weren't. "I think it's cool."

"Ooooh, I like you already," Pearl chortled.

Pearl could just make out the outlines of the three teens. The girl was tall and skinny with long black hair. The two boys were both shorter. One of them also had black hair. Pearl assumed the girl and the boy with the black hair were siblings.

"Do you know where the treasure is buried," the black-haired boy asked.

Pearl decided she liked all three of the teens. If she were young, she would have gone off on a treasure hunt with them. That treasure though was cursed. She felt it her duty to warn them.

"I don't, but I can tell you that if Gertrude had the misfortune of unearthing Brother Twelve's cache of gold coins, then I pray that no one but that rascally pig ever knows where it's buried," Pearl replied honestly.

"Why," the girl squeaked.

"Because, my dear, it's cursed."

"You don't know that," the girl's brother stated.

"Yeah, that's right, you don't know that," the other boy agreed. "There's no such thing as curses."

"Oh, my lovelies, you don't live as long as I have without learning a thing or two. If you were wise, you'd believe in curses," Pearl instructed them. "Brother Twelve was mad. The gold that you're hunting is money that he swindled from his followers. Many of them were left paupers, and some died broken wrecks because of that man. He murdered his wife, scooped out her skull, gold plated it and used it as a soup bowl. There was even talk

123

that when he was young, he captained a slave ship. That gold is tainted with blood and misfortune. Now, you tell me if that doesn't make those gold coins cursed, what does?"

Silence greeted Pearl's words, but she knew it wouldn't last long. The lure of gold was too strong, in the young, and the old.

"I guess it isn't buried on your property then," the black-haired boy said after a time.

Pearl smothered a laugh.

"No, it is not," she nodded, and then took a sip of tea. She winced. She had gotten so caught up in her thoughts that she had forgotten to add milk and honey.

"Well, thanks anyway," the girl chirruped.

Pearl thought the girl sounded like a chickadee, her voice was so sweet and airy.

"You three be careful. I'm sure there are already others out looking for that treasure and they won't be as innocent as you. Men have murdered for far less than the fortune amassed by Brother Twelve."

Pearl heard the teens swallow hard. She had made her point. She doubted that they would listen to an old woman wrapped in a shawl drinking tea with a ghost on her back porch, but maybe...just maybe... her words of warning would make them more cautious.

"Thanks for the warning," the girl said as the little group left, remembering to close the garden gate behind them.

"Mind you don't get sunstroke. It's going to be a hot one," Pearl called to the teens. "If you get dizzy or thirsty, my door is always open."

"Thank you," the raven-haired boy yelled.

Pearl thought she saw them wave goodbye as they continued their adventure but couldn't be sure. She hoped they were waving and not giving her the other sign. They did seem like nice teens.

Pearl rocked. Goosebumps rose on her arms. She pulled her shawl tightly around her shoulders, her hands balling into fists.

She silently cursed the prophet for leaving his gold buried on Seal Island. Deaths would follow. She was sure of it.

Maybe that's why there had been so many bizarre deaths on the island, she thought, startled. *Maybe the Brother's cache of loot was the root of all the evil that had befallen the island in the last few years. As the time of discovery drew near, bad things happened.*

Pearl shivered uncontrollably.

"Jesus, protect those children. They're too young to know what evil lurks in the hearts of men, especially when their brains have turned to mush and their dreams to gold."

***

Morris Tweedsmuir's goats were going insane. They bleated furiously and galloped around the yard like a mountain lion was on their tail. They weren't large goats, except for one old Billy goat that had been in the family for years.

Morris looked out the back door. His herd of brown, white and black Alpine goats were huddled inside the barn. His white milking goats were frantic, racing around the unfenced yard in ever smaller circles. Billy Gruff, the old timer, was no where to be seen.

Morris knocked on Alana's door. It swung open. Her bed looked like it hadn't been slept in. Either she was still following the pot-bellied pig, or she had slept over at one of her friend's homes on the other side of the island. Morris hoped it was the latter.

Morris figured his sister was probably with Melanie. The two had become fast friends in the last year. Reggie was kind enough to let Mel stay on his boat in the summer when he didn't need it since long term rentals on Seal Island were impossible to find during the peak tourist season.

Morris pulled on his gumboots and was about to go see what was disturbing his goats when he heard a single gunshot. It echoed through the forest, the loud report bouncing off the sides of his house.

Morris ran into the living room, unlocked the gun cabinet and pulled a shotgun off the rack. He slipped two twelve-gauge shells into the chamber and pocketed a few more.

He raced out of the house, darting from tree to tree, not sure where the actual shot had come from.

"You idiot, you killed it," Morris heard an angry man shout.

"It was me or him," another man barked back, his Glock pointing at the ground.

Morris raised his shotgun. Billy Gruff laid at their feet, a neat round bullet hole in the middle of the goat's forehead. The goat's yellow eyes were glazed over. His hooves pointed straight out. A tiny trickle of blood dripped down the goat's face from the bullet wound.

"Ya killed my goat," Morris hollered, rage overwhelming him.

He stalked out of the bush, shotgun pointing into the chest of the man who had spoken last.

"Wait," the first man shouted, raising his hands up in the air. "He didn't mean to."

"Ya shot Gruff," the weepy eyed farmer yelled back, pulling back the trigger.

The goat killer started to raise his Glock, but his friend swatted it away.

"Don't! Killing a goat is one thing, killing a man is another."

"Ya should have thought of that afore ya stepped onto my property and shot my Billy," Morris growled.

The men took a couple of steps back.

"Don't shoot," the first man said, "I'm just reaching for my wallet. We'll pay for the goat."

"Oh, yer gonna pay alright," Morris seethed.

"Look, how much for the goat," the goat killer stuttered.

Morris looked over the two men. The men were middle-aged and balding but in pretty good shape otherwise. They wore expensive chinos, touristy t-shirts with 'I'd rather be cruising' and 'Fishing – it's all about how you wiggle your worm' stenciled on the front. Each of them wore one of those new-fangled Apple watches on their wrists.

Morris knew a judge wouldn't give him very much for the old goat, but these two twits didn't know that. The least he could do was make them pay.

"How much ya got," Morris asked, pulling back the second hammer on the shotgun.

Both men rifled through their wallets. Between them they had four hundred dollars.

"Is this enough," the goat killer asked.

"I want that and one of yer watches," Morris grinned evilly.

"That's highway robbery!"

"Then ya can go to jail. No skin off my nose," Morris quipped.

"You shot the goat. Give him yours," the innocent man retorted.

"Fine," the goat killer said, handing over his watch while the other man handed Morris the money.

"What the heck are ya doing creeping around my property," Morris asked them, pocketing the watch and the money. He then lowered the shotgun and carefully un-cocked the trigger.

"Looking for the treasure," the goat killer moaned.

"If there were treasure on this property, ya think I'd be milking goats fer a living," Morris guffawed.

Unbelievable.

"Now, you two get yerselves gone! Go back the way ya came and if ya shoot one more of my goats, it will be the last thing ya ever do."

The two men backed away, their faces red with shame. The one with the Glock put the gun back in its holster.

Morris stood, his shotgun ready, in case they decided to look around some more. He continued to stand there, watching them, and listening to them cuss as they picked themselves up after falling into a tangle of Salal bushes. Salal was thick all over his property. The goats loved it and Morris harvested the berries for jam.

Once the men were gone, Morris sighed heavily. He looked at the dead goat. Tears welled in his eyes as he knelt beside it.

How was he going to explain this to Alana? She loved Gruff.

Morris pulled out his cell phone and started to call Betty. He knew that he should report this. Lord only knows what was happening on the rest of the island

With a start, he realized that there might be a whole lot more treasure hunters running around the island with guns. What if his sister was still following Gertrude and not with Melanie or one of her friends? What if his sister was in mortal danger or worse…tied up somewhere by idiots like these?

He had to find Alana!

Morris hung up and ran back to the house as fast as his legs could carry him.

He'd try Reggie's boat first, and then a couple of her friends. If he couldn't find her, he'd call Betty. She would know what to do.

***

Betty woke up to the sound of her cell phone ringing and a series of sharp raps on the back door.

She rolled off the couch. Her neck was sore, and her muscles cramped. The couch was too short for her or anyone over the age of ten to sleep on comfortably.

"Coming," she yelled as she walked stiffly through the living room to the kitchen to open the back door, the German shepherd padding along quietly beside her.

"Some watch dog you are," she grinned. "Not even a bark, huh."

She opened the door to see her red-faced boyfriend standing there, a cup of steaming hot coffee in each hand.

"How on earth did you get here with those," she asked him, accepting one of the coffee cups, "and they're still hot."

"I drove," he replied cheerily, stepping into the house.

"You have a car?"

"Bought a truck at auction last time I was in the city. It's in yer drive."

Betty did a double take. Reggie was full of surprises.

The grizzled fisherman bent down and gave the dog a giant bear hug. The dog whined happily and licked his face.

Betty laughed.

"Out you go, Champ," she said to the dog.

The dog yawned and then walked out the door as if it owned the world.

Betty noticed that there was already a thick heat haze covering the meadow even though the sun had barely touched it. The top of Watchtower Mountain was also hazy. It was going to be a hot day.

"What brings you here so early," she queried, and then took a sip of the delightfully sweet coffee.

"I figured ya was gonna be busy today," Reggie rumbled.

"Why's that," she said, strolling into the kitchen. She glanced at the clock. It read seven thirty.

"Has yer phone rang yet?" he grinned.

"Yes, but I decided to let you in first," she joked.

Betty watched as Reggie's smile quickly faded.

"It's gonna ring a lot today," he groused. "The buggers are everywhere."

"Who is everywhere? I'm confused already, but then I'm not awake yet either. It was a late night."

"I heard already, about Tammy, I mean, and Tempest's house burning down too."

"Then what are we talking about," she asked for a second time.

"The darned treasurer hunters. They're all over the island. I ran into Morris racing down the road like the Devil was after him. He told me two idiots shot his old goat and Alana never came home last night. That's when I grabbed my truck. We found Alana on my boat with Melanie because Mel was too afraid to be alone. There are crazy people everywhere. The marina is over-flowing. There're people all over the beaches with metal detectors. There's even a news crew interviewing people on the dock."

"I guess I better check my phone then."

Betty checked her cell phone. There was one message. She pressed the dial and listened quietly to the message. Reggie was right. Things were going crazy. After breakfast, she'd call Tom Powder at the main RCMP headquarters in Vancouver.

"Who was it?"

"Frank McDonald. It's the same there. He says there are people brawling on the beach and trying to come up onto the farm."

"Ya know, Bets, this treasure is gonna get people killed," Reggie said, running a hand through his curly grey hair. It was a habitual gesture; one he performed religiously when he was worried.

"Have you had breakfast yet," Betty ventured, wrapping an arm around his waist.

"What did ya have in mind," he chuckled.

"Scrambled eggs and hash browns," she purred.

Reggie looked over her shoulder and saw the disheveled blankets and pillows on the couch.

"Did ya sleep on the couch last night?" he asked, genuinely puzzled.

Betty paled.

"Someone broke in last night," Betty confessed. "They let Gertie and Peaches out. I have to go find them."

"Why didn't ya call me," Reggie growled. "I'd a come over. Did they take anything? What about that coin? They didn't find that, did they?"

"No, the coin was still in my pocket, but they rifled the upstairs. They took a little gold diamond pendant heart that wasn't worth that much, but they made a mess of the library."

Betty instantly knew she shouldn't tell him about the state of the bedroom. Reggie would go nuts. God forbid if he found the thief or thieves that tossed her bed and dresser drawers before she did. He really would turn pirate and make them walk the plank.

"Those buggers," he swore.

"I need to look for the kids," Betty worried, slipping on her runners and heading for the door.

"No ya don't. They're in their stalls. I fed them before I knocked on yer door."

"They are? Well, they were gone when I got home last night," Betty replied, confused.

"Someone must've brought them home then," he nodded sagely. "Maybe yer pa. We'll ask him later."

Betty sighed with relief. She checked her pant pockets at the same time. The coin was still there. She decided then and there that it was going to stay with her wherever she went from that point on.

"Ya know, I hate to say it, but I think we need to look fer that gold," Reggie said. "And we need to keep Gertie close."

"Why on earth would we do that?"

"To try to keep folks from killing each other," he nodded sagely.

Betty couldn't deny that. It was obvious tensions were escalating.

The two of them heard tires on gravel.

They walked out onto the back porch as a pretty young blond-haired reporter bounced around the corner of the house, a red-haired and freckle faced cameraman hustling along behind her. The camera swung around in Betty's direction. Betty found herself staring into the round lens.

"Betty Bruce," the reporter inquired. "I hear your pot-bellied pig has done it again, only this time she's found Brother Twelve's long-lost loot and not a body."

Betty and Reggie exchanged a knowing glance. Neither one of them wanted any part of this.

Champ raced across the pasture towards them, barking loudly.

"Uh, he looks like he means business," the cameraman said, backing away a few paces.

"He does," Betty quipped. "He's my partner. He's got a thing for uninvited guests."

The dog scaled the porch and landed with a thud on the deck.

"And he hasn't had breakfast yet," Reggie drawled.

"How about we come back at a better time," the lady reported stuttered. "Maybe later today."

"Maybe," Betty muttered.

Reggie motioned for the dog to go into the house. The shepherd lowered its tail and immediately scooted through the door.

"And stay out of the barn," she warned the reporter. "None of us have had anything to eat and we've had a long night."

"Oh yeah, someone told us about the guy who got trapped in the chimney," the reporter said, rejoining her cameraman. "Do you know where we can find him?"

"No comment," Betty replied, following Reggie into the house and slamming the door shut behind her.

"What guy in the chimney?" Reggie demanded.

Betty walked into the living room so that she could watch the reporter and cameraman through the bay window. She wanted to make sure they were leaving. She was relieved to see them climb into the big white van parked beside a rusted Ford Bronco, one that looked remarkably like the Bronco she traded in last year. The news crew sat looking at the house for a moment and then finally drove away.

She glanced sideways. Reggie stood there, his eyes intense, his mouth set in a grim thin line, waiting for her to answer his last question.

"Tempe's ex-husband took up residence in the house while she was on her honeymoon. He was on the roof adjusting the satellite disk when he tripped and fell down the chimney, or so he claims," Betty chuckled. "It was quite the sight."

"I thought it was a fire," Reggie queried, his face softening.

"That came after," she shrugged.

"Guys in chimneys, fires, heart attacks, and missing animals, you have had a night," he replied sympathetically.

"I have. Let's have breakfast and then we'll deal with what comes next."

Reggie smiled.

Betty felt her heart flutter. If anyone would have told her that she and Reggie Phoenix would be an item a year and a half ago, she'd have called them a liar. The more time she spent with the grizzled old fisherman, the more deeply in love she fell. He wore his emotions on his sleeve. There wasn't a mean or dishonest bone in his body. He was more than a diamond in the rough; he was priceless.

Champ wagged his tail and looked from one to the other of them expectantly.

Reggie reached down and scratched the shepherd behind the ear until the dog's rear foot went to banging on the floor, the dog's face tilting sideways, a look of sheer ecstasy in the dog's eyes.

Betty chuckled, envying the dog.

And then her cell phone began to ring in earnest.

"Whatever it is, it can wait until after ya've eaten," Reggie growled.

Powder

Inspector Tom Powder arrived with his partner on the late afternoon passenger ferry. They both carried a small over-night bag. Tom had told her that morning that he doubted he could call in reinforcements but would come over to see the mayhem for himself. Perhaps there would be something he could do.

Betty was there to greet the middle-aged Native Inspector. She noticed that his short cropped black hair was a little whiter than when she had seen him last. He had gained a few pounds too but was still a handsome man.

The blond-haired muscle-bound young detective, Ben Hammerton, looked as arrogant as ever. He swaggered as the two men exited the ferry and made their way down the dock towards her.

"Tom," she grinned, walking towards them. "Good to see you."

"And how's that guillotine working for you," she asked Hammerton. Ben had purchased a guillotine from Frank McDonald after Frank had given up on his murder theme park idea once he came down from an LSD induced high.

"I had to sell it to an amusement park. My insurance policy wouldn't cover it," Ben said.

"That's too bad, Ben," Betty laughed. "I'm sure your neighbors are happy though."

Ben shrugged.

"You weren't kidding about the sheer scope of it all," Tom declared, waving a hand towards the packed marina, the crowds of people on the boardwalk, and the overflow spilling out onto the pub's patio. "And good to see you too by the way."

"I thought Tom was joshing when he told me about it," Ben agreed.

The three walked across the landing's parking lot towards Betty's waiting Jeep.

"Hey, new vehicle," Tom noted when Betty stopped in front of the shiny red SUV.

"Bought it right after I sold my condo in Vancouver. I figure this will be the last vehicle I ever purchase, so I splurged," Betty confessed. "I confess I'm still getting used to a vehicle that's smarter than me."

A fight broke out on the crowded patio. Ben took a step towards the brawlers, but Tom stopped him with a look.

"Not our problem yet," Tom cautioned the young man.

Stew and his brother, Pete, emerged onto the patio. Stew picked up one of the men by the scruff of his t-shirt and pinned him against the wall. Pete lifted the other man up like a rag doll and threw him against the railing, bending him over backwards and holding him there, the guy's feet dangling off the ground.

"You boys pay your tab and go back to your boat until you cool off," Stew growled.

"You're hurting me man," said the young man Pete held bent like a pretzel over the porch railing.

"That's nothing like what I'm going to do to you if you don't listen to my brother," Pete threatened.

"Okay," the first young man stammered. "We're out of here."

Stew saw Betty and the two RCMP detectives watching them. He recognized Tom Powder and his partner having gotten to know them quite well last year. He let go of the drunk's shirt with one hand and waved to Betty and the detectives with the other. Even with one hand, Stew had the brawler still pinned to the wall.

Tom and Ben nodded a greeting back.

The drunk tried to break away from Stew. He swung a fist at Stew's head. Stew ducked, grabbed the man's arm, flung him in a circle like a father giving his little girl an airplane ride, and finished with a spectacular crash into the window. Amazingly, the pub window didn't break.

"Come on, pay your tabs," Stew told the two delinquents. He pushed his drunk towards the front door.

Pete let go of the young man he was holding. The brown-haired twenty-something fell backwards over the porch railing and landed with a thud on the ground. The crowd cheered when he wobbled to his feet, apparently unharmed.

The fat man glanced Betty's way. The two made eye contact. Betty didn't like what she saw. He had enjoyed manhandling that boy way too much. Pete grinned sideways, a look of smug satisfaction on his face.

"That fella doesn't look like he likes you very much," Tom noted, his voice flat.

"We've had words," she replied.

"Is there anyone on this island that you haven't had words with," Hammerton joked. He and Betty had gotten off to a rough start.

"Not many," she chuckled. "But I'm working on the rest."

Betty noticed the reporter and her cameraman having lunch in the pub. The woman saw Betty looking at her through the glass window and quickly stood up.

"Time to go," Betty quipped, opening the door to her Jeep.

Betty and the two men got into the vehicle. Powder and Hammerton tossed their knapsacks over the back seat into the cargo space. Betty pressed the start button and threw the car into reverse, barrelling out of the parking lot before the reporter could catch her.

"What was that all about," Tom asked, his head bouncing off the head rest as Betty accelerated.

"Frigging news reporter won't leave me alone," Betty growled.

"Sucks to be famous," Ben laughed.

Betty looked in the rear-view mirror. Ben's gaze met hers. His blue eyes twinkled with glee.

Behind them, the reporter and her cameraman stood on the porch. The woman stomped a foot in frustration. The cameraman tried to calm her down. The pub's patrons laughed and shouted for her to have another beer.

"So where are we going first," Hammerton asked Betty.

"My place," Betty replied. "We'll drop off your bags, pick up Champ, check on Gert and Peaches, and then I'll take you to meet Pearl Tullis. She's the little old lady who may have the answer to Eliza Bone's death."

"Your pig won't try and bite me will it," Ben queried, his smile fading. Gertrude had tried to do some serious damage to him after Ben had accidentally tasered the cow. He had been aiming for the pig at the time.

"Did you bring a taser," Betty queried back.

"No, just my badge, handcuffs, and service revolver."

"Then you should be safe," she said seriously.

Tom chuckled.

Ben grinned.

Tom's chuckles got louder until all three were cackling like a bunch of hens.

Betty pulled up in front of her house.

Champ raced out, tail wagging.

"He sure is a handsome dog," Tom said admiring the German shepherd.

"And he knows it," Betty agreed, turning off the engine.

"So, you had a break-in as well," Tom added as they exited the vehicle and then walked across the yard to the back door.

"Yeah, they were looking for this," Betty replied, pulling the gold coin from her pocket. "I keep it on me at all times."

Tom whistled as he took the coin from her. He examined the Lady of Liberty on the front and the giant golden eagle on the back. He then handed it to his partner.

"And no one has called you to claim it," Ben asked with amazement.

"Nope," Betty retorted, unlocking the back door. "Not even a fraudster trying to claim what isn't theirs."

"I can see why you didn't want Singh involved, at least not right away, but how come you didn't want us to open an investigation and bring over some techs? We could dust your bedroom and the den," Tom asked quizzically.

"Despite all the treasure hunters and tourists here, only an islander would know where I live. I haven't bothered to change the ownership on the house from the estate's name into my name yet. I don't have a land line, just a cell phone. My mail still goes into my father's post office box at the general store. In all honesty, except for moving my clothes in, I haven't done much with the house at all."

"That narrows the field of suspects to a couple of hundred," Ben drawled, handing Betty back the coin. "I thought we got all the bad apples already."

"I guess there are a couple more."

"So, you think more than one person broke into your house?" Tom queried.

"Yes. It's the way they did it," Betty said. "The den and master bedroom were tossed. It was downright malicious. The perp wanted me to feel threatened. I think the perp thought the little diamond heart pendant he stole was something I cherished. My ex-husband gave the necklace to me after I asked him for a divorce. I tried to give it back, but Jim wouldn't take it. It wasn't worth more than a couple of hundred of dollars and I never wore it."

"Ouch," Ben sympathized.

"It's old news," Betty sighed. "The kitchen and living room were searched. The perp who searched downstairs cared. The couch cushions were put back wrong. The stuff in the freezer was also out of order. I keep everything date stamped. I know...I'm a bit of a freak about that. That's how I know there were two people though."

"My wife does the same thing," Tom chuckled. "That date stamping thing drives me nuts. She gets all bent out of shape if I take something newer than the one in front of it."

"You and the missus are back together again," Betty asked, blushing. She felt like she had just cheated on Reggie. She and Tom Powder had almost been an item the last time they worked together.

"Can't you tell," Ben snickered, reaching over to pat his partner's Buddha belly.

Tom grinned and slapped Ben's hand away.

The three sat down at the kitchen table. Tom and Ben placed their bags on the floor by their chairs. The dog sniffed each of the duffel bags.

"You don't have any dope in there, do you," Betty asked the young detective.

Ben rolled his eyes.

Betty still thought the young detective was arrogant, but he had loosened up quite a bit since their first meeting. Maybe Powder was wearing off on him; Hammerton had mellowed considerably. It was either that, or Ben had met a girl.

"You know, Hammerton, you're actually starting to grow on me," Betty told the handsome young detective.

"Ah, that's so sweet," Ben joked

"You're breaking my heart, Betty," Tom cajoled her, a wicked glint in his eye.

Betty snorted in amusement as Tom pulled a notebook out of his pocket and flipped it open.

"While we're here, I've been instructed to arrest Samuel A. Garner for trespass and destruction of property. His ex-wife, Tempest Stewart, has filed charges. He is being very co-operative and is expecting us," Tom said, reading from his notes. "I gather he's staying at his sister-in-law's, one Sadie Stewart. We'll pick him up tomorrow before we leave."

"Tempe decided to press charges, did she? That's too bad," Betty replied sadly. "He's a nice guy. I feel sorry for him."

"Says here that he confessed to the investigator that he was living in the attic," Tom continued.

"Man, that's rough," Ben agreed. "That's why I'm staying single. I told my sister that she should too. She was dating this twit. He had biker tattoos all over his arms and this nasal voice that made you want to cover your ears. Quite frankly, I don't think he had the gonads to be a biker. After I introduced him to Madame Guillotine, he wisely decided to take a powder. No offense, Tom."

"None taken," Tom grinned.

"I'm going to miss that machine," Ben whined.

"I bet you are," Betty chortled.

"Come on, let's check on your animals and go visit the old lady," Tom said, standing up. "What was her name again?"

"Pearl Tullis," Betty answered. "She's half blind from cataracts, but sharp as a whip. She's an interesting woman. You'll like her, Tom. You, I'm not so sure of, Hammerton."

Tom scrawled her name in his notebook.

"So, you aren't setting me up then," Ben grinned.

Betty smirked.

Champ whimpered.

"I was only joking, Champ," Ben advised the dog.

"Time's a wasting let's get it done," Powder said, snapping his notebook shut and heading for the door. Ben, Betty and the dog followed quickly after him.

"I want to turn Gertrude and Peaches out in the pasture before we leave," Betty added. "I can't keep them locked in their stalls forever."

"Can they get out," Tom asked, fixing Betty with a pointed look.

"Not so far," Betty replied.

***

Gertrude watched Betty and the two men drive away, her mouth stuffed with sweet clover. She snorted and squealed her displeasure, nose whiskers quivering in response.

She liked the one man. He smelled of eggs and toast. The pig loved toast almost as much as Milk Bones. She could tell by his voice that he liked her too.

She disliked the other man that travelled with him. He smelled bad. His scent was one of musk and spices. They weren't nice spices either, they were powerful. They made her nostrils burn and her eyes water. A pig never forgets a smell. The musky man was the one who hurt Peaches.

She was not impressed.

The musky man should stay away from Betty and Peaches. She didn't care about the dog. No one had ever asked her about letting a dog live in the house. The dog could fend for itself.

Gertrude spied Peaches in the pasture. Her friend was happily munching on soft marsh grass along side a doe and her fawn. The Jersey cow seemed quite content.

Gertrude wasn't.

She strode purposefully towards the rail fence inside the treeline kitty-corner to the house. The top log rail had fallen to the ground and the fence post that it had been fastened to leaned sideways, its base rotten.

Gertrude arrived at her destination. She looked around. Two more deer, a giant buck and another doe, had joined Peaches and the other deer in the meadow. There was no one else in sight.

She leaned her great bulk against the rotten fence post. It took hardly any effort at all for the post to snap at the base and fall to the ground, taking the two remaining upright cross-rails with it.

She squealed for Peaches to join her. The Jersey cow looked up but then went back to eating, not wanting to go on an adventure today.

Disgruntled, Gertrude stepped over the downed logs and headed off in search of Betty.

***

Morris strode quickly down South Shore Road heading for the landing. He had to find his sister.

Betty pulled up beside him and rolled down the window.

"Where's the fire," she asked him jokingly.

"Have ya seen Alana," Morris stuttered, noticing Inspector Powder sitting in the seat beside Betty and Ben Hammerton in the back.

The dog leaned over Ben's shoulder to get a sniff of Morris. Hammerton pulled the dog back into the seat beside him. German shepherd hair coated his dark suit jacket and trousers.

"I didn't notice her, but there was a tonne of people at the docks and the pub was over-flowing onto the patio as well," Betty responded.

"You sound worried. Any particular reason," Ben asked the agitated man.

"She didn't come home last night, and it isn't like her not ta call or text," Morris said, eagerly covering the truth with a half-lie.

"Reggie told me he saw her on the boat with Melanie this morning. She may still be there; although, I would have thought that Mel would be either working overtime at the pub or at Rainbow and Frank's by now," Betty theorized.

"I'd have thought so too," Morris stammered, deciding to come clean. "The thing is, I ran two fellas off my property awhile ago. The bozos shot Billy Gruff. Thought he was Big Foot or something."

"What," Betty gasped. "They shot your old Billy goat. You should have called me."

"I know, but I made 'em pay for it then and there," Morris replied, puffing out his chest. "I just don't want Alana finding out about it at the pub in case those fellas are down there bragging about shooting my goat. These damn treasure hunters are a curse on the island, I tell ya."

"Sounds like it," Ben agreed from the back seat.

"You sure you don't want to fill in an official report, Morris," Betty asked him earnestly. "They might come back."

"And it'd help us get a couple of constables stationed over here if we have more than one report of theft and disturbance filed by locals," Tom said pointedly.

"I know, I know," Betty shrugged. "I'll file a proper report with Pete Singh. I promise."

"Good. The sooner the better," Tom glared.

"Trespassing and killing someone's livestock is crossing the line in my books," Ben added.

"I got my shotgun loaded," Morris purred. "I know I'm not supposed ta say that, but I ain't letting no more of them kind'a fellas near my place. I'm gonna go see Ida and buy one of her Saint Bernard's off'a her. I'm gonna get the biggest male she'll sell me with the biggest bark to boot. My ole Border collie has run off. I think Max figured they'd shoot him next."

"Okay. If I see Alana, I'll ask her to make sure she calls you, and if I see Max, I'll bring him home," Betty offered.

"Thanks, Bets," Morris said. "You all be careful, ya hear. There's a lot of nutcases running around right now and some of 'em definitely have guns."

Morris backed away from the Jeep.

He watched Betty and the two RCMP detectives drive away. He was glad he told them about those two rich fellas that he snookered into paying too much for the old goat in case they filed a complaint against him. He had thought about telling them about Pete Mann pulling a gun on the drunk college kids, but then he'd have to disclose what he was doing following Pete and Stew in the first place.

Morris walk-jogged down the road, gumboots flapping. He really did have to find Alana. He'd never forgive himself if something had happened to his sister and he hadn't gone looking for her.

After he found her, he was going to take the four hundred dollars and go buy that Saint Bernard from Ida Abercrombie. He hoped four hundred dollars was enough.

The last time he was there, Ida had about twelve full grown dogs and at least twenty puppies running around so he was pretty sure, given the circumstances, that Ida would let one of the dogs go.

Morris slid to a stop.

"Gertie, this ain't a good time to be out and about," Morris warned the pot-bellied pig toddling up the road towards him. He looked around for her cohort, but Peaches was nowhere to be seen.

The pig waddled by him without so much as a backwards glance.

Morris was chagrined. It wasn't like Gertrude not to stop for a visit or to search his pockets for a treat.

"Oh, jeepers, Betty's not gonna be happy about this," Morris worried. "This isn't good. This really isn't good."

He pulled his cell phone from his pocket just as Alana strode up the hill, her long mane of dark red hair whipping about her face as the afternoon wind picked up. You could almost set your clock by that wind, Morris thought.

"Hey, bro," his sister said, waving to him.

"Sis, I've been worried to death," he scolded her.

"Sorry. My phone was dead," she lied. "And you know me and Mel when we get together. We got into the wine last night. You should hear some of her funny stories about the crazies down at the pub. Everyone's all hyped up, thinking they're gonna get rich off'a Brother Twelve's loot."

"That's not the point," Morris scowled. "Ya should'a borrowed Mel's phone and called me."

Alana grinned as she approached her brother.

"Hey, I was pooped. Cut me some slack, bro. I ended up on a wild pig chase over log and over dale. It didn't lead to any treasure, I can tell you that, unless you count pig spit and icky fingers," Alana told her brother. "What about you? Any luck following the Mann brothers?"

"No, they gave up after they were caught snooping around the judge's cottage by a couple of drunk college kids. It was a good thing the fire truck rolled by. That Pete Mann is a piece of work. I thought he was gonna shoot one of those kids."

"Are you serious," Alana exclaimed, her eyes widening in horror.

"Ya think I'd make something like that up!"

"Is that Gertie up ahead," she asked him, abruptly changing the subject.

Morris suspected his sister was still a bit tipsy.

"She's chasing after Betty and the coppers."

"The cops are here?"

"Yeah, same two detectives what were here last year," Morris advised his sister. "I'd have thought you'd have seen 'em get off the ferry. I need to call Betty though and tell her that Gertie's on the loose."

"Oh no, you don't," Alana piped up. "Gertrude's bound to lead us to the treasure sooner or later, with or without Peaches."

Morris bit his lip. He needed to buy a dog from Ida. Should he tell Alana now about Gruff or follow the pig? The island was a powder keg. His sister had no idea how close those boys came to getting shot by Pete Mann last night. That fella scared him.

"What aren't you telling me? You look upset," Alana asked him.

Morris grunted. His sister knew him well.

"Like ya said, there's too many crazies on the loose. I don't want ya going anywhere alone," Morris declared rather self-righteously.

"Oh, bro, that's sweet, but I can look after myself," she hugged him. "Come on, let's go on a treasure hunt."

"Fine, but we're stopping ta get my shotgun first," he drawled.

"Whatever for," she said, astounded by his suggestion.

"Better safe than sorry."

Morris spun on his heel and stomped back the way he had come, his slightly hungover sister in tow.

***

Pete Mann leaned against the railing outside of the pub a pint of Guinness in one hand. He chewed on the stub of a long unlit cigar. Generally, he'd light up just to piss the anti-smoking crowd off. With this many people on the pub's outdoor patio, he had decided to abide by Stew's wishes and not light his stogie. Still, it rankled him. He seldom backed away from a fight, especially one that infringed on his constitutional rights to be a jerk.

He had been moody and out of sorts all day. Last night was a bitter disappointment. It was clear that his little brother had gone soft. Stew didn't have the stomach for what needed to be done to secure the treasure for themselves.

Pete sniffled.

No matter. He could do it himself.

It was his brother's loss.

He had to hand it to Stew though. The pub was a small gold mine in and of itself.

Pete had watched Bruce pick up the two detectives at the dock and drive away. He grinned crookedly, fingering the gold heart and diamond pendant in his pocket. Bet she'd never sleep in her bed again without thinking of him. He grinned, feeling better.

Pete took a long swig of iced cold beer and watched the action unfold in the marina. Boats circled each other in the bay, looking for a place to moor. It was like Christmas at the mall. People shook fists and screamed curses when someone stole a mooring buoy out from under them.

There were scores of people on the beach, scavenging about in either direction, some with metal detectors, others with shovels. It was quite the carnival.

Seal Island had become a mad house over night.

His eyes narrowed when he saw Betty edge her new SUV around a group of laughing teens. She drove slowly up South Shore Road, deep in conversation with her two passengers. Her dog hung its head out the window, tongue lolling, spit dripping down the vehicle's outer door panel.

Pete spat out the end of his cigar and then polished off his beer.

He was about to go into the pub for another pint when he saw the pot-bellied pig trot down the road and then angle south by south-east following after the red Jeep.

Pete grinned and tossed the cigar over the porch railing. Pig hunting, he would go. He stopped in mid-stride when he saw Alana and Melanie stride across the parking lot.

Melanie pushed a blue Norco mountain bike along beside her. The girls stopped in front of the pub, laughed and hugged good-bye. Melanie mounted the bike and pedaled off up North Shore Road. The Morris girl walked right past Pete, totally unaware that she was being watched.

Damn it, he cursed the lithe redhead.

In for a penny, in for a pound, he thought as he pushed his bulk away from the railing and shambled off after the pretty girl and the wayward pig.

Oscars, Flashers, and Old Lace

Betty, Tom, and Ben sat on the back porch of Pearl Tullis' home. Hundreds of bees buzzed inside the giant sunflowers that lined the house and within the colorful array of roses in the garden.

Pearl absently rolled an antique lace doily between her fingers as she lifted her face to the sun. Her face was lined with sadness, her mouth downturned. Her eyes were red rimmed.

Betty could see that Pearl had been crying. Her heart went out to the fiercely independent silver haired woman who sat in the willow rocker leaning forward, ready to speak her truths.

"You know there has been a steady stream of foot traffic up and down the road all day. It started yesterday with a group of teens hiking out on an early morning treasure hunt," Pearl declared. "I warned them to be careful. Remember the Gold Rush? Thousands died and not all by accident."

"The pub and marina are certainly busy and there are more people than rocks on the beach," Betty agreed. "Frank and Rainbow are getting inundated. We'll be stopping in to see them next."

"Oh my, that's awful," Pearl gasped.

"Which brings us to why we're here," Tom said, taking his notebook from his pocket. "My partner and I are the lead investigators on Mrs. Bone's case. I understand you saw her that morning."

"Yes, my friends, Ida Abercrombie and Tammy Smith, and I were there. We had muffins and tea with Eliza…oh, are you sure I can't get you some tea? The Oolong tea that Rainbow brought me is really wonderful."

"No thank you, ma'am, we've had enough already," Ben answered politely.

"You have a wonderful voice. I bet he's handsome, isn't he, Betty," Pearl crooned.

"Yes, he is, Pearl," Betty grinned, "and so is his partner."

Tom and Ben both blushed.

Pearl chortled as she wiped her eyes with a hanky.

"That does make my day," she teased the men.

Tom cleared his throat.

"You were saying."

"Oh, yes, we wanted Eliza's help to convince Tiffany to let us introduce other authors work at the next Seal Island Vagabond Writers Society meeting. Eliza agreed that we should. We had muffins and tea and then left as Eliza had a date. We were halfway down the garden path when I had to use the loo. You see, Tammy and I walked everywhere we could. We walked to Eliza's together and met up with Ida at the foot of Mountain Road. Let me tell you, old ladies squatting in the bush to relieve themselves is not a sight you want to see," Pearl laughed, "so I always make sure I'm good to go before going anywhere."

"I'm sure it's not," Powder agreed, brown eyes crinkling with mirth.

"I don't know if it was easier to pee in petticoats or when we became liberated and started wearing pants," Pearl continued. "Regardless, I prefer flush toilets."

Tom, Ben, and Betty grinned at each other.

"I knocked first, but when Eliza didn't answer, I assumed she was getting changed to go out with Archie, so I just walked in. I was wrong though. I raced past her on the way to the bathroom. She was feeding her Oscars. She was still there, up on her stool leaning over the tank, when I came out. I said 'good-bye', but she didn't answer."

"Did it occur to you that Eliza's not acknowledging you was odd," Ben asked lightly.

Betty shot him a warning glance.

"Why should it? I had already said cheerio and the girls were waiting for me. Tammy gets awfully impatient when I doddle, at least she used to."

"And you're sure there was no one else in the house at the time," Tom asked her gently.

"No, just Eliza and her Oscar fish," Pearl said, her voice cracking. "I only have Ida left now, what with Eliza and Tammy gone. I guess us old gals have to stick together."

Tom closed his notebook. It clicked shut. He reached over and picked up one of Pearl's hands.

"I want to thank you for meeting with us," he said. "We'll talk with your friend, Ida, just to confirm what you said. I am truly sorry for your loss."

"That's very kind of you, Inspector," Pearl whispered, tearing up.

Betty noticed the woman's hanky was wet with tears. She handed the old woman a dry Kleenex.

Pearl pulled away from Tom, accepted the Kleenex tissue and dabbed at her eyes.

Betty was glad that Ben was behaving himself. It was clear that Pearl was the last person to see Eliza alive. Her account of that morning proved that Eliza's death was indeed a tragic accident. Whether or not Pearl could have saved Eliza from drowning in her fish tank had she been able to see better, was anyone's guess. Betty didn't need the young detective to tell Pearl that. Betty was sure the old woman's heart would break if she thought that Eliza might still be alive today if she had had her cataract surgery three years ago.

Betty felt a great weight lift from her shoulders. Pearl's words proved once and for all that her beloved Andy didn't kill anyone. Andy was as much a victim as the others.

"Do me a favor and see if you can find those teens before you go see Ida or Rainbow and Frank. I think they are in trouble. I just can't shake it. It's just like the feeling I had the night Tammy died," Pearl said, turning towards Betty.

"We can do that, Pearl," Betty agreed, raising an eyebrow at Tom.

Tom nodded agreement.

***

Reggie stood up, pushed away from the stool he was sitting on, and stretched. He had been bent over the sample of his new Sleepy Hollow pot line for over an hour. He was developing a new strain, one that would help people deal with extreme anxiety without getting high. It was proving to be a monumental task.

Reggie wandered over to the Oscar fish tank in the corner of the greenhouse. Oxygen bubbles bubbled upwards. Fronds of ornamental seaweed waved at him like the Queen during her birthday parade. Three Oscar fish swam lazily around the giant tank.

Reggie opened the hood on top of the tank and dangled his calloused fingers in the tank, wiggling them slowly. One of the Oscars swam towards him. He gently rubbed the fish's stomach.

"Knew you'd be the first one looking fer a tummy rub, Scully," he crooned.

Reggie pulled his dripping hand out of the fish tank. He dried his hand before picking up a packet of fish food. He shook some of it into the tank. The three large fish made quick work of his offering.

The old fisherman closed the top of the tank and wrote down on a pad of paper tacked to the desk beside the tank what time he had fed the fish. He put the little diary on the desk after one of the fish had died. He suspected it had been from over-feeding. His staff loved to play with the friendly Oscars. Every time they did, they used to feed the fish, hence, the diary. Reggie knew that Eliza Bone, who used to own the fish, would be pleased that the Oscars were so well loved and cared for.

Reggie exited the greenhouse. He stood beneath the overhang he had installed outside the front door after his staff had complained of getting soaked all winter when they went out for a smoke. He stood in the doorway for a moment inhaling the warm fresh air.

Something moved in his peripheral vision.

He did a double take as he saw Gertrude streak by the entrance to his driveway, heading towards the top of South Shore Road.

He was about to call Gertrude when he saw Alana and Morris race after her. Morris held a shotgun loosely in one hand. Morris' gumboots and t-shirt flapped loosely on his gaunt frame. Alana was beautiful, as always.

Reggie felt the heat rise into his cheeks.

He liked both the Tweedsmuirs, had known them all their lives. He knew exactly what they were doing. They were hoping Gertrude would lead them to the treasure.

Reggie strode quickly toward his cottage. He kicked off his gumboots and tugged on a pair of old sneakers. He turned towards the road in time to see Stew's brother creep by. The fat man kept to the shoulder of the road so that he could hide quickly if he had to.

The old fisherman scowled. He tucked his fish knife into his belt. There was no way that he was going to let Stew's brother hurt either of the Tweedsmuir siblings. Not in this lifetime or any other. The idea that Pete might have it in for Gertrude didn't even occur to Reggie.

***

Gertrude slowed down, her attention diverted by a couple of golden Delicious apples resting against a Mars bar wrapper and a large clump of crumpled cellophane at the side of the road.

"Look at that! The bloody tourists are dumpin' their garbage left and right," Morris growled. "I'd like to catch 'em at it. I tell ya, I'd make 'em pay."

"No, you wouldn't," Alana chuckled. "You don't have a mean bone in your body."

"I didn't mean I'd hurt 'em," he whined, "I'd make 'em pick it up though."

Alana grinned. That was the brother she knew, not the one who was toting a shotgun for no good reason.

"That looks like Betty's Jeep up there," Alana pointed down the road to where a red 4x4 was parked in front of Pearl Tullis' house.

"Ah, shite," Morris swore. "That's where Gertie's goin' then. This has been a wasted effort."

"Nothing is wasted, bro. I learned that at college."

"Speakin' of which, ya are goin' back in September, right?"

"We'll talk about that later," Alana said.

"Oh no we won't," her brother glowered, placing one hand on his hip since the other hand contained a loaded twelve gauge.

"Seriously, Morris, later."

Albert Albert, also known as Also Albert, took that moment to leap out from behind a purple leafed Smoke bush, holding open the lapels of his black leather duster, his fly open, a foot long fake penus extending straight out from between his legs.

When Albert 'Also' Albert realized there was more than the pretty red-haired girl standing in front of him, her look of shock turning into a look of sheer delight, he fell backwards, his black felt top hat sailing into the bushes, the fake penus flapping from side to side like a pendulum.

"What ya doin' flashin' my sister with that thing," Morris shouted, raising the shotgun.

"Don't shoot me, mister," the terror stricken young man begged.

Alana burst into a gale of laughter, her whole body shaking so hard that she almost fell on top of the helpless young man tangled up in the purple Smoke bush, the rubber penus pointing at her like the teacher used to do with his finger during math class when she didn't get the question right.

Alana had never been good at math. It was why she didn't want to go back to college, not to be an Administrative Assistant where she was expected to learn bookkeeping.

The young man looked up at the smiling goddess who pushed the man's shotgun out of his face and smiled back.

"Stop it, Morris, he's harmless."

Gertrude picked the golden apple off the ground and started to eat it, yellow green slobber dripping from her mouth, watching the goings on with interest.

"Gertie, look what you've gotten us into," Alana scolded the pig.

The pot-bellied pig grunted, then picked up the other apple.

"GERTIE," Betty yelled angrily as she and the two detectives jogged down the road towards the Tweedsmuirs and Albert 'Also' Albert.

"We caught us the flasher," Morris hollered back, yanking the trembling young man to his feet.

Also Albert stared down at his sneakers. They were black Reeboks with a bright pink rim and pink laces. His crisp white shirt was no longer white, the front of it mottled with dirt and leaf debris, the underarms wet with sweat. His black leather duster was equally as dirty.

Alana reached into the bushes and picked up Also's top hat. She brushed off the dust and leaves and gingerly placed it back on top of Also's head.

The look of gratitude in the poor fellow's face made her heart ache for him.

"Who have you got there," Tom panted as he arrived on the scene.

"Dunno, Inspector," Morris replied, giving the boy a shake. "Never seen him before."

"What about you, miss," Ben asked Alana.

Alana opened her mouth to answer, but then glanced sideways at the rubber dick hanging loosely between the young man's legs. The fake willie was broken and unable to stand to attention as it had previously. In fact, the foot-long wiener now resembled a short hockey stick. Alana burst into another hysterical fit of laughter.

Also's face broke into an angelic smile.

Ben assessed the young man, the innocent aura about him, the broken willie flopping between his legs, felt top hat, and leather ankle length duster, and tried not to laugh. He absently rubbed his chin, trying to hide his wide grin.

"Gertrude," Betty said, wagging a warning finger at the errant pig, "bad pig. You shouldn't be here."

Tom fought to keep a straight face. "What's your name, lad," he asked the young man.

Also Albert's eyes suddenly brimmed with tears. His face blossoming with shame.

"Albert," the young man stuttered.

"Albert what," Tom inquired.

"Albert," Also Albert replied.

"You don't have a last name," Betty continued, not half as amused as everyone else seemed to be.

"No. Yes. That is my last name," the young man squeaked.

"I thought you said your name was Albert," Tom said, puzzled, and then to Morris, "You can let him go, Mr. Tweedsmuir."

Morris let him go, but purposefully raised his shotgun, cocking the trigger and aiming it at Also Albert's crotch.

"Put away the gun, sir," Ben ordered Morris.

Morris blushed, furious, but let the gun drop to his side, the barrel facing the ground.

"Again, is Albert your first or your last name," Tom asked the young man.

"It is," Also replied with a sniff.

"I got it. Albert is your first and last name," Alana gushed, clapping her hands like she'd just won a new car on *The Price is Right*.

"Yes," Also grinned.

Tom took out his notebook and scribbled down the young man's name.

"My Auntie calls me Also," the boy said to Alana.

"You don't hear that every day," Ben snickered.

"That's enough, Ben," Tom warned his protégé. "And I don't want to see you wandering around with that shotgun ever again, Mr. Tweedsmuir, even if you feel you have a reason to."

Morris blushed an even deeper shade of red. Wisely, he did not answer.

Alana saw a knowing look pass between the Inspector and her brother. She wondered what that was all about.

"Also," Betty inquired. "Why are you doing this?"

"Auntie told me that I'd make the ladies laugh," Also replied earnestly.

"Ya thought that jumpin' out of bushes and flashing women with a rubber dickie would do that," Morris asked, flabbergasted.

"Also meant no harm," Alana said, rising to the boy's defence. She suspected Also couldn't be more than eighteen, his face was so full, open and earnest.

"Auntie said it was funny," the boy blabbered, more tears falling.

"Albert, do you have any family here on the island," Betty asked nicely. "Who is your Auntie? Do you live with her?"

"Yessum," Also nodded. He wiped his nose on his sleeve. "I just wanted people to like me. Auntie's lady friends all laughed when they saw me."

"What ladies," Tom pressed, eyeing Betty.

"Auntie's ladies," Also said again, looking up into the Inspector's kind eyes. "Auntie told me where they lived. She said I wouldn't get into trouble."

"Again," Betty asked gently, "who is your Auntie?"

"Auntie Ida," he said with a grin. "She's got lots of puppies. I love the puppies. They clean my face after dinner."

"Oh, no," Alana gasped.

"Pretty lady would love the puppies," Also said coyly to Alana.

"Ida Abercrombie? I was just gonna go see her," Morris mumbled. He whistled under his breath. "Huh! What're the odds, eh."

"Why were you going to see Ida," Alana asked, turning on her brother.

"To buy a dog," he whispered.

"What?"

"To buy a Saint Bernard," Morris confessed. "I didn't want ta tell ya like this, but some rich dudes lookin' fer Brother Twelve's loot shot Billy Gruff. I planned on getting' us a watch dog, something big and imposing, so I thought I'd go get one of Ida's. Max took off. I don't know where he's gone."

Alana started to cry. Morris folded his arms around his sister.

"Don't cry, miss, Also can make you happy," the young man said, opening his arms to join in the Tweedsmuir siblings hug. "I know just the dog for you."

Ben caught Also by the arm and gave the boy a warning look. Also backed away knowing exactly what that look meant.

"How about we drive you back to your Auntie's, Also," Betty suggested. "You can ride in the back seat with the detective and my dog. You'll like Champ and I'm quite sure he will like you. We'll have a talk to your Auntie Ida about your little adventures and who she sent you to see to spread the joy. Maybe later you can help Morris and Alana pick out a new dog."

"Okay," Also agreed. "I like dogs."

"Where did you get that," Ben grinned, pointing at the rubber dickie.

Alana shot the detective a curious glance as she broke away from her brother.

"Hey, Halloween's not that far away and I lost my guillotine," Ben said to Alana.

"You're the one who bought Madame Guillotine from Frank?"

Ben grinned.

Alana grinned back.

"We'll try and get Gertrude ta go home," Morris offered with a sideways glance at his sister. Instinctively, he raised the shotgun.

"Morrissss," Betty hissed.

Alana punched Ben playfully on the arm.

Gertrude heard her name and looked up. She saw the bad man standing beside the interesting man with the pink funny thing dangling between his legs and squealed.

"Oh, no!" Betty exclaimed.

Gertrude charged.

Ben and Also Albert stumbled backwards. They tripped over each other's legs and fell, one on top of the other, into the Smoke bush that Also had recently risen out of.

Morris tossed the shotgun aside and leapt onto the attacking pig. Morris had forgotten to lower the trigger. The gun went off, spraying buckshot into the neighbor's garden.

KABOOM!

Betty dashed in between Gertrude and the downed detective and Albert 'Also' Albert.

Tom dodged around the medley of angry pig, Morris's feet, Betty's outstretched arms, and the frightened men writhing on the ground, like a star quarterback. He picked the double-barrelled shotgun off the ground and emptied the chambers.

Betty's German shepherd jumped through the open side window of the Jeep and raced to the rescue.

***

Pete Mann peeked out from behind the cedar hedge of the neighbor's property, watching the goings on down the road.

He pulled a cigar from his pocket.

All this sneaking about for what? The darned pig wasn't making it easy.

Pete hated that pot-bellied pig. Once it showed him where the treasure was, he swore he'd shoot the nasty thing.

Pete felt a tap on his shoulder and turned around. Towering over him was an irate giant of a man with piercing grey eyes, a scruffy grey beard, and gnarled hands the size of a catcher's mitt.

"What ya think yer doing skulking around in the bushes," the man growled menacingly.

"Watching that crazy pig attack a cop," Pete replied mildly, holding his temper in check.

"Really?"

"Really," Pete responded, refusing to be goaded into action. "Didn't you hear that gun go off."

"Oh," Reggie grumbled, suddenly unsure of himself. "I didn't know it was a gun blast. Thought maybe it was kids playing with cannon crackers."

Pete knew the tall man: Reggie Phoenix, pot-grower, retired fisherman, and Bruce's boyfriend.

Pete grinned. He could be nonchalant and friendly when required.

The joke was on Phoenix and Phoenix didn't know it. Pete had rifled through his girlfriend's bedroom.

Pete's smile widened even more.

Reggie's expression softened.

Pete wanted to laugh in his face but thought better of it. He was out for a walk…that was it.

"You better stay back here with me," Pete said amiably. "It's safer."

Reggie glanced down the road to where Betty and Morris were struggling to haul Gertrude off Ben Hammerton and a young man dressed in black. Tom Powder held a shotgun under his arm. Champ was barking furiously and dancing all around them.

"It appears so," Reggie agreed. "Ya didn't answer my question though. What're ya doing here?"

"Can't a man go for a walk without getting accosted," Pete replied, indignant.

"Just a walk, is it?"

Pete patted his belly.

"My doctor told me I had to lose weight."

Reggie grunted and backed away.

There was a loud squeal and a terrified scream.

"Geez," Reggie cussed. "I gotta go. I just want ya ta know that I'll be watching ya. I knows what yer up to. I ain't no fool."

Reggie spun around and jogged away.

Pete lit his cigar and took a long drag. He fought the urge to linger. He hoped the cop on the ground's partner would shoot the pig. He doubted it would go that far but a man could hope. For some reason, people seemed to like the dirty boar.

Pete took another hit off the cigar, closed his eyes and enjoyed the rush of nicotine.

After a moment, he opened his eyes and began walking back to the pub.

The sun beat down on his shoulders, the heat making his face drip with sweat. A cold pint of Guinness was in order. He could almost taste it.

Later, he'd hear about the day's events. Someone was sure to fill him in. They always did.

***

Reggie seethed. He knew Stew's brother was lying. People took him for slow, but Reggie was anything but. He thought things through, is all.

Reggie suspected that Pete Mann was the one who broke into Betty's house. He prayed that if Betty was right and there had been two burglars, that Stew hadn't been the second one. They were friends. The betrayal made Reggie feel sick.

Reggie ran as fast as his old knees would allow towards the ruckus in the street, his mind revving at a pace far quicker than he was able to run.

He got there just in time.

Gertrude sent the slim farmer flying. He landed with a thump on the gravel shoulder of the road. The German shepherd nipped at Morris' heels thinking he was a threat.

Reggie wrapped Gertrude's head in an arm lock as she rounded on Ben Hammerton, ready to charge him again. He pulled the pig's head around to face him.

"Gertie, that's enough, ya here me," he ordered the pig.

"Champ, break!" Betty screamed from somewhere to his right.

Gertrude's breath was hot on his cheek and smelled of apples.

"Oh, Reggie, thank God," Betty hissed, helping him push the pig away from the downed detective.

Tom pulled first Ben and then Also Albert to their feet. The dog nosed the young man, tail wagging.

Gertrude whipped her head out of Reggie's grasp. The shepherd skipped sideways. The pig sunk her teeth into Also's fake willie and ripped it off the leather thong that was holding it to his pants.

Also wailed in protest.

The dog whimpered and slunk towards him, tail down. Champ licked the boy's hand trying to make him feel better. Also wrapped his arms around the dog and hugged him to his chest.

Gertrude turned sideways, dodging right and then left, evading Reggie's and Betty's outstretched hands as they tried to catch her. She bolted away, her stubby legs threatening to buckle under her weight as she ran, her hooves clattering on the hard-packed gravel road, what was left of the pink plastic willie hanging from her mouth.

Gertrude floundered, her legs giving out, and plowed face first into the road. She quickly picked herself up and continued down the road, past Betty's SUV parked in front of Tammy Smith's driveway, towards the deer trail at the end of the road.

"What on earth was that thing," Reggie gasped, breathless, watching the pig disappear into the forest at the end of the road.

"A fake willie," Betty huffed.

"Oh, well, that explains it then," Reggie muttered, eyeing Betty.

The two grinned at each other.

Champ rushed over and planted a wet kiss on Betty's face as she leaned forward, hands on her knees, catching her breath.

"Hopefully Gertrude will stay out of trouble for the rest of the day," Tom grinned, offering Reggie his hand.

"Don't hold yer breath," Reggie grinned back, shaking the Inspector's hand. "And I'm glad ya didn't shoot her with that thing."

"Oh this," Tom said, lifting the shotgun. "It's empty."

"Are you okay," Alana asked Ben.

"I'm okay," Ben assured her, taking a step towards the pretty redhead. "That pig hates me though. She sure can carry a grudge."

"You're the one who tasered Peaches," Alana chortled.

"Not my finest hour," Ben confessed.

"A trigger-happy twit is what ya are," Morris stuttered, tugging his sister away from the handsome police detective.

Ben and Alana's eyes met. The chemistry between them was palpable. It filled the air with electricity.

Morris danced between the two, furious.

Tom, Betty, and Reggie exchanged a knowing glance.

Also Albert sniffed, his tears flowing once again as he held what was left of the giant willie.

"How am I gonna make the ladies laugh now," Also cried.

Champ rushed over to him. He licked the boy's tears away.

Old McDonald's Farm

Frank and Rainbow McDonald stood on the bank above the high tide line watching people scramble back to their dinghies and inflatable boats as the tide rushed in.

The cove's beach was steep. When the tide came in, it came in like a lion.

Several groups of treasure hunters stood on rocky perches looking bewildered as the water collapsed the holes that they had dug in the sand only moments before, effectively cutting them off from the trail they had used to get to the McDonald's formerly private little cove. The trail was only usable at low tide.

"We should leave them there," Frank grumbled, noting that two of the stranded people were Bermuda shirt and his mouthy female companion. "Serve them right."

"You know we can't do that, honey," Rainbow said, her brow knitting together as she watched three teens paddle in circles in what appeared to be a slowly deflating dinghy.

"How are we going to help any of them," Frank replied. "We only have two kayaks."

"They're not who I'm worried about, Frank. I think those teens out there are in real trouble," Rainbow said, pointing at the teens in the flimsy inflatable boat.

The blow-up boat was being pulled sideways into the strait instead of into shore by a cross-current. The two boys paddled, one on either side of the boat, but they only made things worse, working against each other instead of together. The sides of the rubber dinghy were quickly collapsing. The girl was panicking, frantically waving her arms in the air. Her gestures made the boys more agitated. One of them lost his paddle.

The other boats had already sped away around the point, leaving the teens alone.

"They don't have lifejackets," Frank said, alarmed.

"What were they thinking?"

"They're kids, they don't think," Frank muttered angrily.

"We have to get to the kayaks," Rainbow cried.

"Yeah, you're right. Run up to the barn and get our lifejackets and paddles and I'll haul the kayaks down to the beach," Frank told her, quickly realizing the teens were going down...and going down fast.

Rainbow kicked off her floppy sandals and raced up the sandy path to the barn to get the paddles and lifejackets.

Frank bolted across the grassy bank. He unfastened the ropes that tied the twin florescent orange Necky kayaks to the wooden rack and then hauled them down to the beach.

Rainbow reappeared wearing a bright yellow lifejacket, her dreadlocks bouncing. She carried another two red lifejackets, one old and threadbare, but still functional, as well as two double bladed kayak paddles.

"Get in and I'll push you off, babe," Frank told his wife.

"I've got one spare lifejacket," she said.

"Great. The strongest swimmer of the three can wear that," he said as he dropped his wife's kayak into the water. "We can get the other two to hold onto our boats and we'll pull them in."

"That water's still pretty cold," Rainbow worried.

"Nothing we can do about it," Frank said. He gave his wife a quick kiss and pushed her off. "We'll just have to do our best."

"Hey, help us," Bermuda shirt yelled from the rocky knoll that he and his wife were stranded on.

"You'll have to wait," Frank hollered back as he buckled his lifejacket. He was thankful that they had left the dog in the house. Blue would have drowned trying to save the kids.

Frank hauled his kayak into the water, dropped it in, slipped inside the cockpit, and shoved off. He paddled furiously after his wife.

Frank quickly caught up.

The tide pushed against the plastic hulled boats, forcing Frank and Rainbow to dig deep. Their kayak blades dipped and sliced through the ocean waves.

A hundred yards away, the dinghy collapsed. The teens fell into the water.

"Help," the girl screamed, her long dark hair plastered to her face. "My brother can't swim!"

The girl's brother sputtered and flayed his arms, trying to dog paddle, but it was useless. He quickly slipped under the water. The strong current dragged him under the collapsed boat.

The girl and her companion dove underneath the waves.

"I'm calling 911," a stranded tourist yelled from the rocky promontory.

Frank heard him but knew it wouldn't do much good. The Coast Guard were too far away. It was up to him and Rainbow. He ground his teeth and paddled harder, his kayak shooting past his wife's. Fear gripped his breast when the teens didn't surface.

"Rainbow, don't you dare leave your boat to try and help them," he hollered at his wife, seeing her jaw set into that stubborn line he was so used to seeing when she set her mind to something. "I can't rescue all of you at once."

"What're we going to do," she screamed back.

"Pray, baby," Frank answered, his pulse racing.

Suddenly, the girl and taller of the boy's heads popped out of the water. They dragged the unconscious dark-haired boy out from beneath the boat. The two struggled to hold him afloat.

Frank pushed forward with all his might, the kayak skimming over the water. He turned swiftly, digging his paddle deep and using it as a rudder. He pulled up beside the teens.

"Don't all jump onto the kayak or we'll roll," Frank advised the two teens. "See if you can push him onto the front of the kayak and I'll roll him over."

"Here, this will help," Rainbow cried, throwing the worn lifejacket to the girl.

The girl tugged the lifejacket over her shoulders. With the help of the older boy, they managed to do up the frayed buckles while simultaneously trying to keep the other teen from drifting back underwater.

"He's not breathing," the girl bawled, spitting out a mouthful of salt water.

"Push him up on his belly," Frank said, reaching over and grabbling hold of the boy under the armpit.

The teens grunted and pushed the boy over the front of the kayak. The teen was dead weight. The kayak dipped and wavered. Frank reached over and rolled the teen over so that he was on his back, the teen's bum sinking into the front of the kayak's cockpit atop of Frank's legs.

Frank grit his teeth. He let go of his paddle, the paddle leash fastened around his wrist keeping the paddle from floating away, tugged the boy's face towards him and began CPR.

"You, without the life jacket," Rainbow commanded the boy in the water, "grab onto the back of my kayak. "Don't watch my husband. Focus on me."

The boy in the water shivered, his lips turning blue. He grabbed hold of the back of Rainbow's kayak and held on.

"Do you think you can swim to those rocks over there," Rainbow said to the girl.

"I think so," the girl stuttered, her teeth chattering.

"Think or do?" Rainbow asked her.

"I don't know," the girl whined, her teeth chattering. Even in the summer, the water in the strait was cold.

Rainbow grabbed her tow rope and threw it to the girl.

"Tie that around your waist," Rainbow ordered the girl while Frank continued to perform CPR by rolling the boy's head to the side to remove excess water from his mouth. Frank then leaned over and blew four strong breaths into the unconscious boy's mouth and then pressed his hands over the boy's upper chest and pumped up and down rhythmically four times and then repeated the process.

Rainbow turned back to the girl, pushing the image of Frank performing CPR on the boy out of her mind. The girl's fingers were clenched into claws, the skin white and swollen with cold. The girl finally managed to tie the rope around her waist and give Rainbow a thumb's up.

Rainbow turned the kayak around and paddled hard, the blades slicing into the water. Her shoulder and arm muscles screamed. Rainbow battled against the extra burden. She would not let these kids die. It was a good thing the tide was in her favor.

"You can do it," Rainbow heard the young couple stranded on the point yell.

"Stroke. Stroke. Stroke," another man hollered.

Rainbow didn't have time to look. The weight of the boy on the back of the kayak was crippling her ability to tow the girl in.

"Swim, girl," someone called, cheering the young girl on.

"Kick your feet boy. Help her out," the young couple urged the boy.

"When are you gonna come get us," screamed Bermuda shirt. "That kid out there is done for and we're up to our ankles now."

Rainbow ignored them and powered on. She could feel the two teens trying to help as the drag on the kayak lightened.

She glanced over her shoulder and saw that Frank had stopped CPR. The teen lay with his head on Frank's shoulder, feet in the water, coughing up salt water. She grinned and pushed on.

The kayak's hull scraped against sand and rock.

Rainbow hauled herself out of the kayak and splashed into the water. She helped the boy to the beach and then hauled the girl in the rest of the way.

Rainbow collapsed on the beach beside the two teens.

A chorus of cheers erupted from the stranded people.

"Rainbow," Frank gasped, paddling his kayak into shore.

Rainbow staggered to her feet and half pulled and half lifted the boy off Frank's kayak. Frank slid effortlessly out of the cockpit and helped Rainbow carry the boy the rest of the way into shore.

The girl threw herself at her brother, sobbing with gratitude.

"Thank you so much," the girl cried.

"The old lady warned us. She said that treasure was cursed," the brown curly haired boy said. "I didn't believe her."

Rainbow and Frank wrapped their arms around each other in a fierce hug. Tears flowed down both their faces.

Around the point came two silver skiffs, Archie Bruce and a local fisherman in one, and Stew Mann in the other.

The men angled the skiffs into the point, expertly maneuvering around the coral and sharp rocks to pick up the people left stranded by the tide.

"I'm really cold," the girl shivered.

"Meeeeee toooo," her brother stuttered.

"Ditto," said the other boy, blowing on his hands.

"I'll go get some blankets," Frank said, breaking away from his wife's embrace. He gave his wife a quick kiss and then ran up to the house.

Rainbow squatted down beside the girl. She rubbed her hands up and down the girl's shoulders, willing warmth into the stressed-out teen. She thanked the Universe that it was summer, and the air was a balmy; otherwise, the outcome for these three could have been much worse.

Frank returned with the blankets, Blue galloping across the trail in front of him.

A Coast Guard hovercraft rounded the point, engine's roaring. It came to a stop. Once it was safe, Stew and Archie angled their boats up to the ladders the crew tossed down. Coast Guard members then helped the people the men had rescued off the rocks onto the hovercraft.

"You guys can come warm up at our place and then we'll take you home," Rainbow said to the teens as Frank wrapped a wool blanket around each of their shoulders.

"My dad is going to be so mad at me," the curly haired boy said.

"I think your parents are just going to be happy that you didn't drown," Frank consoled the boy.

"You don't know my dad," the boy whimpered.

"Don't worry, I'll talk to him," Frank consoled the boy.

"Next time you go out on a boat, especially an inflatable, make sure you wear lifejackets, right," Rainbow added.

The teens nodded in unison.

"Look at it this way. You'll have one heck of a story to tell when you go back to school," Frank grinned.

The teens smiled, the color returning to their faces, the blue tinge in their lips from hypothermia receding.

Blue took that as his cue to jump from lap to lap, rolling over on each one for a tummy scratch.

"There's nothing like a tummy scratch to make you feel better," Frank laughed.

"Ours or his," the raven-haired girl asked.

That brought on a new gale of laughter.

"I'm glad Stew rescued that rude man and his wife," Rainbow whispered in her husband's ear.

"Cheeky, cheeky," Frank chuckled, hugging his wife close.

They both watched in amusement as the man in question started yelling "I'll sue!" at Stew when Stew cupped his hands under the man's wife's bottom and pushed her none too gently up the ladder and onto the hovercraft.

***

Gertrude jogged down the trail to the beach. She then turned inland, ignoring the strange scene that was going on in the cove with people shouting and hollering at each other as the tide rolled in. She broke down to a walk, her legs and hooves sore from the pounding they had taken.

She strolled into the meadow and sighed with relief. The meadow was much cooler, the giant oak, maple and fir trees that shaded it providing a welcome canopy of green.

She ambled past the sod hut with the broken door and collapsed against the trunk of the ancient oak. She nosed at the hole that she had dug days before when she was looking for truffles. Something gold glinted in the soil.

She nuzzled the gold coin. It smelled sour. Just to make sure it wasn't really a tasty treat, she bit into it. The metal tasted fowl and she spat it out, indignant.

Unfazed, Gertrude closed her eyes and rested, letting the ocean breeze cool her skin, and the sound of the wind in the trees lull her to sleep.

It had been a long night without much sleep and her search for Betty had left her exhausted.

When she was rested, she'd dig around under the tree a bit to see if she could find some truffles.

A long white and black nose poked out of the doorway to the old sod cabin. The white and black nose connected to a white and black head which was attached to a Border collie named Max.

Max's nostrils quivered.

He recognized that smell.

With a wag of his tail, he crept out of his hiding place. He trotted over to the pot-bellied pig that lay sleeping beneath the shade of the oak tree.

Max circled once and then twice before laying down beside the pig, leaning his slim body against the pig's back, comforted now that he had a friend for company.

Saint Bernard's & Sister Fate

Pete Mann walked casually along the side of the road. He was on the long sloping bend that connected Mountain Road with South Shore Road. South Shore Road turned into North Shore Road at the landing. Pete thought whoever named these roads had no imagination whatsoever.

Betty's Jeep slowed as it passed him. Betty rolled down her window as she drove by. She lifted a hand half-heartedly and waved. It was a limp wave at best.

An angelic looking boy wearing a black top hat waved energetically at him from the back seat.

Pete waved to the boy, his face breaking into an uncharacteristic wide-mouthed grin. He couldn't help himself. The boy shined.

A German shepherd, its face squashed up against the tailgate window stared at him with cold eyes.

Pete had forgotten about the dog.

He had the distinct feeling the shepherd had caught his scent through the open window and recognized it. That wasn't good.

Oh well, Betty couldn't prove Pete was in her house. He had worn gloves...no prints...no proof. He had no intention of fencing the little pearl necklace in his pocket. It wasn't worth much. The retired cop had annoyed him when he first met her. He had stolen things from people for far better reasons, but few were as satisfying.

Pete knew he wasn't a good man. His brother and he used to be cut from the same cloth, but somewhere along the line Stew had changed and grown a conscience.

The Jeep turned right on Mountain Road, its wheels spinning in the loose gravel.

Pete was glad to see its taillights disappear around the corner.

He heard voices behind him and turned to see Morris Tweedsmuir and his sister striding down the road. He hadn't realized that he had dawdled that much on the way back to the pub.

They walked by him, deep in whispered conversation, with a brief nod of acknowledgement.

Pete noticed that Morris no longer carried the shotgun. He chuckled. He suspected it was in the back of the cop's car.

He pulled a stubby box of port tipped cigarillos from his pocket, unwrapped the cellophane wrapper, and tossed it aside. He pulled out one of the cigarillos and lit up.

He inhaled, enjoying the sweet taste of port mixed with tobacco.

He watched silently as the Tweedsmuir siblings also turned right up Mountain Road.

He stopped and turned back to face up South Shore Road, expecting to see Phoenix walking towards him. Pete could see his driveway from where he stood.

Interesting, Pete thought.

No Phoenix!

Pete took a deep puff from the cigar and let out a smoke ring. He reached around his back and fingered the small gun holster that rested there, hidden beneath the folds of his shirt.

He grinned and started walking back the way he had come. He was sure that Phoenix was following the pig, secure in the knowledge that it would lead him to where the gold was buried. Pete intended to be there when it did.

***

Reggie hummed a Gordon Lightfoot tune as he marched up South Shore Road to retrieve Gertrude.

"The searchers all said, they'd have made Whitefish Bay if they put fifteen more miles behind her," he sang softly, unable to help himself. He loved Lightfoot's *The Wreck of the Edmund Fitzgerald*. It seemed fitting given what was going on.

What a strange day, he thought as he strode forward, humming the rest of the song. He wished that he and Betty could just grab Champ, a couple bottles of wine, some supplies, and head north up the strait. The taste of the sea on his lips, the smell of diesel fuel in his nostrils, and the feel of Betty beside him, was all he needed to be a happy man.

Life had gotten complicated.

Reggie was a simple man.

There were too many people here. They were despoiling his island…and then there was the matter of Stew's brother, Pete Mann.

Reggie believed in evil. He couldn't say for sure that Pete was evil, but he wasn't good either. There was a darkness about him. It wasn't that he was over-weight or slovenly, in fact, he dressed well and had an air of 'money' about him, but Reggie doubted that Pete Mann had ever performed a hard day's work in his life.

An eagle cried overhead.

Reggie glanced up.

The white-headed Bald eagle circled above him, its wings outstretched, catching the air current, its keen eyesight searching the ground below.

Reggie felt his heart soar; his mood lifted.

The road he walked on ended in a turn-around, but the deer had created their own highway through the greenspace between South Shore Road and the McDonald farm. The greenspace was a public right-of-way. One deer trail meandered northeast, ending at the upper reaches of Mountain Road while a second trail branched into two, one branch finishing at the top end of the McDonald farm and the other branch circling around to the beach.

Watchtower Mountain was a provincial park. You could reach it by parking at the end of Mountain Road and climbing up the unmaintained trail that wound through the forest to the blunt peak. It wasn't a tall mountain. Reggie thought of it more as a hill than a real mountain, but he was an expert mariner, not a geologist.

Reggie reached the end of South Shore Road and took the deer trail to the right, heading for the beach that bordered the McDonald farm. This was the shorter route home for the wayward pig since the McDonald farm's entrance was on North Shore Road, on the far side of Watchtower Mountain.

Reggie smelled the ocean before he reached it. A smile creased his lips.

He stopped on the beach to admire the view in time to see the Coast Guard hovercraft preparing to exit the narrow cove. He shaded his eyes from the sun. Two boats pulled away from the hovercraft, the aluminum skiffs being tossed about as the wind whipped the waves into a three-foot chop. He couldn't see who was manning the skiffs.

The hovercraft waited for the two skiffs to round the point before firing up. The hovercraft's engines were deafening as it inflated its balloon like floats and skimmed over the water, heading for the main island, or so Reggie assumed.

"Probably some idjits caught by the tide," his deep voice rumbled. He shook his head in disgust. Treasure hunters! Ugh!

Reggie started walking along the beach. With a start, he stopped short.

"Now who's being the idjit," he growled, and reversed direction, heading back up into the woods.

There was no point in going directly to the farm without first checking the hermit's decrepit homestead and the surrounding meadow. It would save him a long walk back.

Reggie broke through the brush, startling a couple of grouse. They flew deeper into the forest, their wing beats creating a soft whistling sound.

Reggie watched the birds until they disappeared and then walked purposefully towards the small one room sod roofed log cabin nestled amidst some poplars beside a rock outcropping.

He hadn't been there in years.

Reggie was about eight years-old when he met the hermit who lived in the sod cabin. He and his father were fishing off the point when the old man beckoned them to shore, asking if his father had any tobacco to spare. His father, being a good-natured man himself, had rowed to shore and offered the strange fellow some pipe tobacco. The memory flooded back to him.

How couldn't it?

Reggie's eight-year-old mind had conjured up images of Merlin. The hermit looked like a sorcerer. The old man's beard and long hair were scraggly, his white cotton slacks and thigh length shirt as white as his hair. His dark brown eyes were intense, his skin as bronzed as that of the local Natives. He was both exotic and foreign in nature.

The man refused to answer his father when he asked the man his name. Thereafter his father referred to the strangely clothed old man simply as *The Hermit*.

Before they left, *The Hermit* said to Reggie: "Take heed of the boar, young man, and beware the fatted calf for his soul follows not the path of the Great White Lodge."

The words chilled Reggie to the bone. Even now, his arms blossomed with goosebumps. He had never told anyone about that meeting, nor had his father to his recollection.

Reggie moved the door to the sod cabin aside and took one step over the doorstep. He peered into the gloomy open space.

Cobwebs hung from the ceiling. Mice and rat droppings littered the floor. A hand-hewn wood table and a couple of spindly chairs stood by the window. A broken china basin, a clay pitcher, and some mottled tin cutlery rested on a tall trestle table beside the table. There were a few rusty tins of corned beef and some old marrow candles on a shelf beside that. A single bed made from short poles and cedar boughs stood against one wall, the cloth and goose down mattress atop it had been decimated by moths and mold.

The air was cool but infused with the scents of rot and decay.

Across the room was a huge cedar chest, its wood darkened with age, the leather fasteners green with mold, the brass clasps stained black. Reggie thought briefly about opening the chest but then remembered his mother's favorite saying about curiosity killing the cat.

He backed slowly out of the cabin.

Reggie continued his search.

He walked around the far side of the cabin.

"I see ya found a friend, Gert," he chuckled, striding towards the pig sleeping in the shade, Morris' Border collie stretched out beside her.

Max lifted his head and wagged his tail.

Gertrude opened her eyes and grunted.

"Ya certainly caused yer mum some grief today," he scolded the pig lightly. "And you've got yer pa worried sick, Max."

Reggie stood over the pig and dog, a grin spreading across his face, his grey eyes sparkling with mirth.

"And I see ya been diggin' fer truffles again," the rugged fisherman said, looking down at the hole Gertrude had dug beneath the tree roots.

"What's this then," he said as something gold winked at him from the bottom of the hole. Reggie used a stick to push the slime covered remains of Also's plastic willie aside and reached in to pick up the gold coin.

The Border collie ran to him, tail wagging furiously.

"Not now, Max," Reggie said, pushing the dog's face out of his. "Well, I'll be."

Reggie whistled, examining the gold coin. It was definitely the same as the one that had become lodged in Gertrude's hoof.

He noticed bits of a broken mason jar and a metal lid in the deep impression in the earth. He used the same stick to brush the dirt from the glass and saw the glitter of gold in the black earth beneath it.

Reggie drew in his breath. His heart beat wildly in his chest like a trapped bird.

He quickly pocketed the coin and filled in the hole with loose dirt and leaves until the indentation was barely visible.

Gertrude grunted and heaved herself to her feet. She trundled up to Reggie and snorted in his face.

"Ah, Gertie, that was a nasty thing ta do."

The dog wagged its tail and politely licked Reggie's face clean. Reggie pushed the dog away once again and put a hand on Gertrude's back, using her broad girth to help him to his feet. He brushed the dirt from his jeans and reached into his pocket, tugging out a short piece of twine.

"Well, it ain't a dog's leash, but it's gonna have to do," he said amiably. "Max, you can either go home or come with me and Gertie to the farm."

Reggie wrapped the twine around Gertrude's neck and tugged her forward.

The dog barked out a warning.

"You aren't going anywhere," a gruff voice said from behind him.

Reggie spun around. Stew Mann's sweat-soaked brother faced him, the small calibre revolver in his hand pointed directly at Reggie's chest.

***

Alana and Morris Tweedsmuir arrived at Ida Abercrombie's sprawling acreage to find the cherub faced senior, the two RCMP detectives, Betty, and the top-hatted Albert 'Also' Albert, sitting at a rose patterned iron table in the back yard drinking iced tea while Betty's German shepherd played dodge ball with a dozen adorable Saint Bernard puppies of various ages.

Several exuberant adult dogs galloped towards them, drool flying, ears flapping.

"Oh, my goodness, I'm in love," Alana crooned as a bunch of puppies broke off from the pack surrounding Champ and raced over to her, tails wagging.

"Which one," Ida laughed.

"All of them," Alana answered, falling to her knees to be smothered by puppy kisses.

"I hear you need a dog, Morris," Ida said.

"Aye, I do," Morris grinned as a six-month-old puppy as big as the German shepherd jumped up and licked his face, leaving a slug like trail of spit in his beard.

"I told Auntie that you wanted a dog," Also hollered, running towards Morris.

Also grabbed Morris by the hand and pulled him over to meet an older female Saint Bernard with a mostly white face, and a black and brown saddle on her back. The dog lazed happily in the shade, watching the other dogs cavort around the yard.

"This is Mazie," Also said, bending down to pat the dog.

"Mazie," Betty queried.

Morris tugged his beard out of the friendly pup's mouth. He turned towards Betty, surprised by the irritated tone in her voice. Her face was creased with worry. Her eyes were shadowed, dark circles beneath them. She looked shell shocked, rather like she had after Andy died. No one else at the table seemed to notice.

"Yes, I named her after Tiffany's fictional detective, Mazie Owens," Ida confessed, a sheepish look creeping over her face. "I think I've been suitably chastised enough today though; don't you think?"

"There's always room for more," Betty threatened.

"Mazie is, was, one of my first breeding females," Ida informed Morris. "She is seven years-old. I spayed her two years ago. She was a wonderful mother, but it was time to retire her bloodline. Also is right. She would be a perfect watch dog for you."

"Does she have a big growl on her," Morris asked, liking what he saw. The dog was reserved, and calm compared to all the others.

Mazie stood up, yawned and then extended her nose to sniff the goat farmer. She looked into Morris' eyes with a keen intelligence.

Morris grinned. He turned to his sister to ask what she thought, but she was still busy rolling on the ground with the pack of dogs.

"Saint Bernard's don't growl. They bark and they bite, but seldom do the last one," Ida sniffed. "In fact, I've never heard of it. Certainly, none of mine have."

"They are gorgeous dogs," Tom Powder said. "I'm thinking of taking one of the puppy's home. My kids have been bothering me to get a big family dog. The wife's terrier was a nasty little thing. She was all bite and no bark, passed away a couple of weeks ago. I hate to say it, but my wife's the only one who misses her."

"I guess that other matter is all taken care of," Morris asked questioningly, nodding towards Also.

The young man rolled over and over in the grass until he was head to head with Alana, puppies jumping all over the two of them.

"Also has promised to never play any more practical jokes on anyone no matter what his Auntie says," Betty replied flatly, her eyes downcast.

Morris wondered what was wrong. It sounded like everything had been dealt with. He hadn't been happy about the kid flashing his sister, but his temper was short lived. Under the circumstances, he was relieved that the boy wasn't going to be arrested.

"And I pinky swore," Also said with a laugh as a vibrant pup dive bombed him.

"He did that," Ben chuckled.

"So, does that mean yer gonna give me my shotgun back, Bets," Morris asked, his hand roving over the smooth coated Saint Bernard's back.

"Nope," Betty said, glaring at Morris.

"Guess I deserved that, but that's my best bird huntin' gun," he whined.

"It's in the back of my Jeep. You can grab it when you leave," Betty said, "but it's empty and going to stay that way until you go bird hunting in the Fall."

"Yes, ma'am," Morris agreed, knowing there was no point arguing with Betty anyway.

"Are ya really willing ta part with Mazie here," Morris asked Ida.

"I can, or you can take that big bear over there," she said, pointing to a gigantic male who had decided to play tag with the German shepherd whether the shepherd wanted to or not. "His name is Brutus."

Alana finally peeled herself off the ground.

Brutus loped towards her, tongue lolling, spit flying, his pace ground eating. The other dogs scattered before him.

"Do you want an inside or an outside dog," Ida asked Morris. "Mazie is used to being inside the house. She sleeps on the couch. Brutus, on the other hand, is a going concern. He's definitely an outside dog."

"I think we should take Brutus," Alana laughed, wrapping her arms around the hundred-and-fifty-pound dog's head.

"I think yer right, sis," Morris drawled. "Sorry, Mazie."

Mazie flopped back down on the ground, unconcerned.

"What do ya want fer him," Morris asked, worried that he couldn't afford the dog.

"Don't worry about that. We'll settle up another time," Ida chuckled and waved a hand nonchalantly in the air. "Take Brutus with you. Keep him for a few days to make sure that you are all a good match. There's a chain leash by the front gate. He hasn't much training on him, so he'll be very strong on the leash."

"Well that's darn right neighborly of ya," Morris said, feeling the heat rise to his cheeks.

"I know he's going to fit right in on the farm," Alana crowed, fetching the leash from the hanger beside the gate as Saint Bernards of all sizes gallivanted after her.

"What does he eat, Ida? I feed Max a pink salmon and potato mix mostly," Morris asked, realizing for the first time how big Brutus really was. The dog outweighed his sister by a good forty pounds.

"Don't worry, if he's really hungry, just feed him one of your goats," Ida joked. "Or two."

"What," Morris stuttered.

"I was just kidding, Morris. He's a good dog with a wonderful temperament. Salmon and potato are fine. That's what's in the dry kibble I feel him. Call me later if you have any questions."

Too late, Morris realized that Alana and Brutus were already gone. He knew where they were though. Ida's pack of dogs galloped along the property's fence line marking Alana and Brutus' progress as Brutus dragged her down Mountain Road at breakneck speed.

"I better go," Morris yelled, alarmed.

"Make sure you lock the gate behind you," Ida called after Morris.

Morris heard the hearty sound of laughter as he ran to catch up with his sister, totally forgetting to retrieve his favorite twelve gauge from the back of Betty's SUV.

***

Betty smiled crookedly as Champ and the other dogs continued to race back and forth along the fence line of Ida's acreage, tracking Alana, Brutus, and Morris' progress.

"Are you really serious about taking a puppy home," Ben asked his partner.

"Yeah, I'm betting the ferry personnel are used to animals," Tom grinned. "And funnily enough my wife and I had talked about getting another dog last week. Of course, we were thinking Labrador, but she's going to love a Saint Bernard."

"You do have a big yard," Ida queried. "These aren't apartment dogs. Despite my offering Mazie and Brutus to Morris on the spot, I do vet where and who takes one of my Bernard's home."

"I have an acreage," Tom said. "My family home is in Squamish. I didn't want to raise my kids in the city. I keep a small studio apartment downtown for when I'm working long hours."

Ida nodded and picked up her glass of iced tea.

"Which one would be the best family pet? I have two girls, twelve and nineteen, a ten-year-old son, and a six-month-old granddaughter who lives with us."

"Bernadette would be perfect," Ida said, pointing towards a four-month-old bundle of joy who had become fixated on Champ and was following him everywhere. "Three of the others are already sold. They are just waiting for their new owners to come pick them up now that they have had their last shots."

Betty smiled for a moment and then turned away to study the slice of lemon in her iced tea, effectively blocking out the rest of the conversation.

It was the right thing to do, not arresting Albert 'Also' Albert for flashing Alana and the two old women, but it was heartbreaking as well.

Also had told her that Pearl had invited him in for milk and cookies after he had flashed her his fake willie, runaway, and then returned later to apologize. Betty truly believed that Pearl had called her about the flasher before Also come back to make amends. Pearl should have phoned Betty back to let her know about it but didn't. Betty guessed that Pearl didn't want to spoil the joke on Tammy. Seal Island residents weren't known for their forward thinking or 'normal' behaviour.

She could confront Pearl, but it served no purpose. Pearl hadn't had a premonition that something bad had happened to Tammy. She already knew it had when Tammy hadn't called her to laugh over Ida's practical joke.

As for Ida... Ida was not without blame.

Also told his Auntie that her friend, Tammy, had fallen down laughing. The boy didn't understand that the woman had probably laughed so hard that it killed her.

The whole episode was out of a Shakespearian tragedy, one that in this case was all too real.

"What do you think of Bernadette," Tom asked Betty, startling her out of her reverie.

"I think she's a love-bucket," Betty grinned, the puppy's gentle eyes and plush-ball face rescuing her from the dark tunnel she was spiraling into.

"Do you mind if we bring her back to your place for the night so she can sleep beside me and get used to me before we take her on the very long ferry ride home?"

"No problem," Betty replied as Champ laid his head in her lap, looking up at her with beseeching eyes. "And no, Champ, we aren't bringing a puppy home for you."

"Are you sure," Ida giggled. "I think he's in love."

"A German shepherd, a pot-bellied pig, and a Jersey cow are enough of a handful for me, but thanks for the offer," Betty declared.

"I see your point," Ida conceded.

"Can we pick Bernadette up after dinner. We still have to go out to the McDonald farm and drop by Sadie Stewart's to make sure you won't have any problems with Sam Garner, Tom," Betty asked Ida, but was looking over at Tom.

"That would be fine," Ida purred. "I'll have a puppy pack ready for you, Inspector Powder. There will be a leash, a collar, some organic dog shampoo, pooper scooper bags, and enough puppy food for a week. You do have a good-sized vehicle on the other side, don't you?"

"I have a suburban," Tom grinned.

Betty thought Tom looked like a little boy who had just been offered the last piece of a Dairy Queen ice cream cake.

"This should be fun," Ben quipped, eyeballing the rambunctious puppy.

"She can sit on your lap on the drive home," Tom advised his partner.

"Oh, no, she won't," Ida exclaimed. "You'll be stopping at the nearest pet supply store to buy a crate after you get off the passenger ferry."

"Yes, ma'am," Tom agreed. "I just wanted to see my partner's face."

"All right gentlemen let's rock n'roll," Betty chuckled.

Prophets & Prophecies

"Hand it over," Pete demanded, holding one hand out. He leveled the gun, aiming it directly at the tall man's heart.

"Hand over what," Reggie glowered, seemingly unfazed by the gun toting man.

"The gold," Pete sighed, not surprised that the retired fisherman didn't even blink at the weapon pointed at his chest. He had been a pot smuggler after all.

"I know you have it or know where it is."

"If I did, I wouldn't tall ya," Reggie growled.

Beside the broad-shouldered man, the pig snuffled, her beady eyes looking at the ground, her nostrils quivering.

"The pig says different," Pete replied, pointing his gun at the freshly disturbed ground.

"Don't know nothing about pigs, do ya," Reggie snorted with amusement. "They're always hungry. Gertie's just lookin' fer grubs."

The Border collie lay beside Reggie's feet, out of the way of Gertrude's hooves. The dog panted, its ears swivelling back and forth.

"That your dog," Pete nodded towards the Border collie.

"Nope, don't own a dog," Reggie replied flatly.

"Whose is it then?"

"Don't know," Reggie lied.

Now he had something to threaten the man with, Pete thought.

"You're a terrible liar, Phoenix," the fat man grinned.

The dog sat up, scooted its bum around, ears springing to attention, as it focused on a sound coming from the forest behind them that only a dog could hear. The dog started to tremble with excitement.

A faint thrashing sound came from somewhere up the wooded trail beyond the clearing.

The dog woofed and trembled harder.

"What's with the dog?" Pete asked.

Reggie shrugged.

Gertrude pawed the ground, her hoof pushing away the leaves and soft packed earth.

"Gertie, stop," Reggie commanded the pig, but Gertrude ignored him.

The sound of bleating sheep filled the air.

"Go get 'em, Max," Reggie whispered fiercely to the collie.

The dog bolted into the woods.

"That wasn't very smart," Pete threatened. "Get down on your knees and join the pig. Dig up my treasure or I'll kill it."

"Not with that pea-shooter you won't," Reggie growled. "All yer gonna do is piss her off. Gert knows how to deal with shites like you. Ya think I'm scared of ya? Ya think Gertie is? She's killed men fer less."

"You're stalling," Pete said, looking around. "There's no one here to help you."

The earth started to shake.

The bleating of sheep and the sound of a dog barking got louder and louder. This was followed by the sound of an even larger dog barking.

Gertrude continued to dig, oblivious to the small earthquake that was filling the hole up with dirt as fast as she was digging.

***

The herd of wild sheep came hurtling through the bush, the Border collie nipping at their heels. The dog circled behind them, driving them forward, down the small incline and through the mounds of Salal that grew beneath the stand of evergreens and deciduous trees.

The sheep burst out of the forest, veering right past the pot-bellied pig and the tall grey-haired giant, bleating with terror.

At the same moment that the sheep tried to dodge around the fat man standing a few paces from the grey giant, a great monstrosity of white, brown and black tumbled out of the bush.

The sheep panicked.

They bolted straight into the fat man.

Pete struggled to stay upright as the sheep knocked him from side to side, almost taking him out at the knees. He thought he was safe until the Saint Bernard sent him flying, happily joining the Border collie in its effort to drive the sheep forward.

The gun went off!

Ka-pop!

The bullet ricocheted off the tree beside Reggie's head and then veered off into the forest.

Reggie leapt into action, tackling Pete Mann in mid-air as Mann struggled to his feet.

Alana and Morris raced in, breathless from their run down the road in pursuit of Brutus.

"Get that twine from around Gertie's neck," Morris ordered his sister as he jumped into the fray.

Alana ran over to the pot-bellied pig, unwrapped the twine from around Gertrude's neck, and then barreled back to where her brother and Reggie had managed to flip Pete Mann onto his belly.

Reggie held the fat man in a tight headlock. Morris pinned the man's hands behind his back. The gun lay some distance away.

"Tie his hands up tight," Morris hissed through gritted teeth.

Alana circled the twine around the downed man's hands, making sure to tie the twine tight. She tied the twine as tight as she could without drawing blood.

"Owww, that hurts," Pete yelled.

"Ain't that a shame," Reggie muttered.

Brutus came bouncing back upon the scene, his tail wagging, his ears and face soaked with drool. The dog's eyes shone with happiness.

"Brutus, come," Alana called to the dog, satisfied with her handiwork.

The dog bounded towards her.

Max, upon hearing Alana's voice, trotted back from the beach, his tail also wagging.

"Max," Morris shouted, letting go of Pete Mann. "Good boy."

Max raced up to Morris and licked his hand.

"Get up," Reggie growled, half-lifting the former treasure hunter and thief to his feet. Something gold fell out of Pete's pocket.

Alana bent down to pick it up. It was a gold heart with a diamond stud on a little gold chain hanging from the middle of it.

"What's this," Alana asked.

"That's the thing that's gonna put this here fella in jail fer even longer," Reggie grinned.

Morris bent down and picked up the revolver. He looked at the small pistol.

"This ain't the gun ya had the other night," Morris blurted out.

Pete's eyes narrowed.

"What ya talkin' about, Morris," Reggie asked quizzically.

"Tell him, bro," Alana urged her brother.

Morris sighed.

"Alana and I was lookin' fer the treasure and thought we'd follow Gertie, but the Mann brothers beat us to it."

"Or so we thought until we heard Peaches and Gertrude down on the beach by the pub," Alana interrupted.

"Let me tell it," Morris chastised his sister.

She shrugged and hugged the Saint Bernard, picking up the short chain leash that hung from his collar.

"Anyway, Alana went down ta the beach and I followed after Stew and this fella. These college boys thought ta do the same thing. This idjit pulled a gun on 'em, but it wasn't this gun. It was bigger."

"Is that so," Reggie said, shaking Pete, trying to get an answer from him.

"That's not my gun," Pete wheedled. "Doesn't have my prints on it."

Morris dropped the gun.

Alana rolled her eyes and picked up the little revolver.

"I like the feel of this," Alana grinned, and then pointed it at Pete Mann.

"Yeah, give me that," Morris growled, swiping the little gun from her grasp.

Ka-pop!

The gun went off again, the bullet burying itself into the dirt at Pete's feet.

Everyone jumped, including the Saint Bernard. Max raced for home.

"Lordie, put that thing away," Reggie yelled.

"Sorry, Reg," Morris apologized.

"Hey, what's that Gertie's found," Alana said, pointing at the hole the pig had re-dug.

Gold coins glittered inside the hole and in the earth mounted along the sides. Two mason jars stood unbroken, rolled aside, as Gertrude dug wider and deeper in her search for black truffles. The rotted sides of a wooden crate were visible and another row of mason jar lids.

"So, this is where the prophet buried his loot," Reggie drawled, his voice cracking with emotion.

"Well, don't just stand there, get the gold," Pete gasped as all three people stood silently looking down into the hole.

"We found the treasure," Alana crowed.

"I'm not touchin' it anymore than I have ta," Reggie mumbled.

He looked from one person to the other.

"It's cursed," Reggie added.

"It's not cursed," Alana chortled, her eyes widening.

"Oh, yes, it is," Reggie said, fixing Alana with a pointed look. "That there belonged to the hermit who lived in that sod roofed cabin. I know now that he was Brother Twelve. He told me: *Take heed of the boar, young man, and beware the fatted calf for his soul follows not the path of the Great White Lodge.* I understand what he meant now."

"Are you calling me a fatted calf," Pete sniggered.

"I'm just repeatin' what the prophet told me."

"Reggie's right, Alana," Morris agreed. "I've changed my mind. With all the death and violence on the island that's been happening since Gertie found that darned coin, I agree, those coins are bad luck."

"Seriously, bro, I have a hard time believing that," Alana said, torn between wanting to walk away and taking at least one of the jars of coins for herself.

"Don't listen to them," Pete pleaded. "Cut me loose and we can all share it. Those coins are worth millions."

"Alana, would ya give a million dollars to have Gruff back," Morris said, looking his sister dead in the eye, "because that's what that gold has already cost us."

Alana reached into her pocket and pulled out her cell phone. She kissed the Saint Bernard on top of the head and then dialed a number.

"What are you doing," Pete whined. "Don't bring any more people in on this.

Reggie and Morris smiled.

Alana put the cell phone on speaker and then handed Reggie Betty's necklace and pendant.

Reggie stuffed it in his pocket.

The cell phone continued to ring.

"Bruce, here," said the woman on the other end of the line as she answered the call.

"Hey, Betty, I think you better drive back to the end of South Shore Road," Alana spoke calmly into the phone. "And bring that handsome detective with you. Tell him I need his handcuffs. Oh, and a shovel. Definitely bring a shovel."

Reggie and Morris burst out of laughing.

Pete Mann was not so amused.

Gertrude didn't care. She had found a rotting truffle.

Desolation Sound

Betty and Reggie sat in deck chairs watching the half moon rise over the water. Behind them the horizon was a blaze in purples and pinks as the sun disappeared for the night behind the mountains at their back. A camp lantern sat on the deck, illuminating the wooden deck of the *Persephone*.

Betty took a sip of red wine, savoring the mixture of berries and grapes in the fruity bouquet.

Reggie stared off into the distance, his eyes hooded with tiredness, a half-full can of Kokanee resting on the deck beside him.

Champ lay on deck, his feet moving, his lips flapping as he chased a rabbit in his dream.

The boat was motionless, the water beneath was calm. They were moored in a quiet cove with no one else nearby to disturb their peace.

It had been an exhausting three weeks.

The press had hounded them at every turn until they decided to disappear on the trawler in the middle of the night, leaving a brief message for Archie and Violet letting them know that they would be back in a couple of weeks. They had taken Gertrude and Peaches to Frank and

Rainbow's farm with the promise that Frank not let any reporters take any more pictures of Gertrude.

For once, even the pot-bellied pig had tired of all the attention and seemed content to chase a chicken around the yard whenever she got the chance.

Betty got her pendant back. Pete Mann was arrested on numerous charges from theft, breaking and entering, to assault with a deadly weapon. He refused to implicate Stew in the burglary of her house, and Stew hadn't confessed to being a part of it. Betty and Reggie knew the truth and it broke both their hearts. Maybe one day, they could forgive Stew for his betrayal, but it wouldn't be any time soon.

As for the necklace, Betty hated it. She ended up giving it to Alana as Alana had expressed an interest.

"Do you think Alana will ever forgive you for donating all that gold to charity," Betty asked her boyfriend, thinking that the heart shaped pendant had looked really pretty fastened around Alana's neck.

"She'll get over it," Reggie replied softly. "She's got a new dog and a new beau to keep her busy. I think she'll be good for that young detective. Maybe he'll retire that chip on his shoulder. I also think that even the Brother would be happy with the outcome."

"That's right, he was a sea captain once upon a time, wasn't he," she said, admiring the moon.

"He was," Reggie agreed. "That money will help out a lot of military and maritime widows."

Betty turned towards him. His grey beard and curly hair shone with an unearthly light for a moment and then the affect faded. It must have been a trick of the moon and the lantern glow, she supposed.

"Ya know, I went back that night," Reggie confessed, raising his head and gazing over at her.

"To where?"

"The cabin."

She reached a hand towards him and he gripped it tightly. His callused palms and fingers twined around hers.

She waited, patient, with all the time in the world. The man she loved would talk when he was ready and not a minute before.

Somewhere in the dark, a fish jumped.

It was followed by the bark of sea lions.

Champ whined, still chasing that illusive rabbit in his sleep.

"I took all the stuff out'a the trunk. It's packed away in a box in the closet at my place. I didn't want no reporters or treasure seekers findin' it."

"What're you going to do with it," she asked quietly.

The world went unnaturally quiet. It felt like every living thing inside their little corner of the universe had stopped and was listening to what Reggie was going to say next.

Betty tossed back the last of the wine in her glass.

"When life is back ta normal, I'm gonna donate it ta the museum in Nanaimo. There were some personal diaries inside the box. Tidal charts too. They were close ta fallin' apart, but ya could still read them with a magnifying glass," he said, his voice as hushed as Betty's had been.

"Anything else?"

"Merlin's robe," Reggie replied.

"Merlin?"

Betty thought Reggie was blushing, but it was too dark to be sure.

"Yeah, a wizard's robe. It had stars and moons on it. There were some old clothes like they wear in the Middle East too. Ya know, the stuff that looks like pajamas."

"Huh," Betty exclaimed, humbled.

Reggie had told her about his meeting with *The Hermit* when he was a boy. It had been a long time ago.

Wait a minute, Betty gasped, letting go of Reggie's hand. Reggie had told her he was fifty-eight.

"Reggie, the marker in the cemetery you showed me with the name of Edward Smith on it that you said was *The Hermit* read that he died in 1953. You went to high school with me for a few years so how can that be? How could you have been eight years-old when you met Brother Twelve and still go to high school with me?"

"Well, ya see, Bets, one of the reasons that my father and I never talked about meeting the Brother ta anyone is because we already knew that he was buried in the church cemetery. No one would have believed us if we told them our story."

Betty felt the blood drain from her face.

Reggie continued, his baritone voice rumbling like thunder in the mountains as it grew stronger and more earnest.

A whale breached off to starboard, so close that the air from it blew out of its blow hole sounded like a gunshot.

Betty jumped.

Reggie continued calmly.

"Ya know the teachers thought I was a slow learner," he laughed. "I just wanted ta see ya every day fer as long as I could before one of them figured out that I wasn't as daft as they thought I was."

"Say again?"

Reggie stood up. He offered Betty his hand. Betty took it and he pulled her out of the chair and into his arms.

Once again, Betty saw a soft aura of light surrounding him.

"I love ya, Bets, always have, always will," he whispered gruffly in her ear. "Ya've always been all the treasure I need."

The End

Brother Twelve's gold has never been found despite the hundreds of treasure seekers who have searched the countless islands in the Pacific Northwest looking for it... then again, maybe it has?

Stay tuned for more adventures with Betty and Gertrude in Chasing Santa.

If you enjoyed this novel, please consider leaving an honest review on Amazon, Bookbub or Goodreads.

Why leave a review?

Reviews help readers find books and discover amazing new stories. It only takes a minute of your time to leave a review and it means a lot to the author.

For more information on Laura Hesse, this series, or to learn about upcoming releases, simply hit the "follow me" button on:

Publisher's website at Running L Productions

Interesting Links – More on Brother XII

If you would like to find out more about the incredible and bizarre story behind Canada's first cult and the prophet Brother XII and Madam Z, then click on either of these links to documentaries or read John Oliphant's novel titled Brother Twelve which is available on Amazon.

TV Show 1965 (great show with interviews with people who knew Brother XII and the lawyer from his trial):

https://www.youtube.com/watch?v=X9ARwMCxXiU&fbcl id=IwAR0Is7ITil7VZI2AEIg35PjPSFVvT-pnWcIhRZU76vaumR_c4D8UmyCtkXk

Historica Canada:

https://www.youtube.com/watch?v=U5MG6xUQlCQ

Book: *Brother Twelve* by John Oliphant

Article: https://bcbooklook.com/2016/03/09/178-edward-arthur-wilson/

Novels by Laura Hesse

Children/Fantasy:

Gus, The Flood, The Unicorn King, The Unicorn & The Dragon, The King of Christmas and *The Unicorn Wears Red*

The Holiday Series:

One Frosty Christmas, The Great Pumpkin Ride, A Filly Called Easter, Independence and *Valentino*

Paranormal Thriller: *The Thin Line of Reason*

The Gumboot & Gumshoe Series:

Book One: *Gumboots, Gumshoes & Murder*
Book Two: *The Dastardly Mr. Deeds*
Book Three: *Murder Most Fowl*
Book Four: *Gertrude & The Sorcerer's Gold*
Book Five: *Chasing Santa* (Coming Soon November 2020)

Non-fiction & Comedy/Adventure:

The Silver Spurs Home for Aging Cowgirls
Peter Pan Wears Steel Toes

If you want to find out more about Laura Hesse or hear about her upcoming releases, then visit www.RunningLProductions.com and hit the "Follow Me" button or follow Laura on Goodreads, Amazon or Bookbub.

About the Author

Laura lives on the west coast with a rescue dog and two old cats. She grew up a backstage brat in Music Hall Theatre and credits her mother with her love of song and theatre.

Laura spent many happy years riding the trails and writes about the special horses in her life within the pages of her young adult series of equine novels. While Sally and all the rest have passed over the rainbow, they will forever live on in her stories.

When not writing or researching her next novel, readers may spot Laura kayaking out on the water somewhere or camping at a nearby park.

Made in the USA
Coppell, TX
31 August 2020

35865740R00120